She'd taken far too many liberties.

But the moment of ire was brief.

Katie and his little girl looked so right lying there together. A woman with a big heart and strong convictions and a child who had lost her mother.

Katie was worming her way into his house, his heart, his child's life.

He had to put a stop to this. He couldn't be the hero Katie wanted, the hero she needed. He couldn't take a chance of leaving his child alone in the world, he couldn't risk...

Risk. That's what it amounted to. Terrible risk.

He left the room with a heavy heart. When Katie woke up he'd have to be firm, he'd have to make her understand. He'd get her to safety and that's all.

For now, he'd be her protector. Beyond that, he could do no more.

ALICE SHARPE

DUPLICATE DAUGHTER

HARLEQUIN®

TORONTO • NEW YORK • LONDON
AMSTERDAM • PARIS • SYDNEY • HAMBURG
STOCKHOLM • ATHENS • TOKYO • MILAN • MADRID
PRAGUE • WARSAW • BUDAPEST • AUCKLAND

This book is dedicated to Katherine Jones, Hayden Jones
and Carmen Sharpe, with everlasting love.

ISBN-13: 978-0-373-88703-3
ISBN-10:   0-373-88703-5

DUPLICATE DAUGHTER

Copyright: © 2006 by Alice Sharpe

www.eHarlequin.com

Printed in U.S.A.

ABOUT THE AUTHOR

Alice Sharpe met her husband-to-be on a cold, foggy beach in Northern California. One year later they were married. Their union has survived the rearing of two children, a handful of earthquakes registering over 6.5, numerous cats and a few special dogs, the latest of which is a yellow Lab named Annie Rose. Alice and her husband now live in a small rural town in Oregon, where she devotes the majority of her time to pursuing her second love, writing.

Alice loves to hear from readers. You can write her at P.O. Box 755, Brownsville, OR 97327. A SASE for reply is appreciated.

Books by Alice Sharpe

HARLEQUIN INTRIGUE
746—FOR THE SAKE OF THEIR BABY
823—UNDERCOVER BABIES
923—MY SISTER, MYSELF*
929—DUPLICATE DAUGHTER*

*Dead Ringer

CAST OF CHARACTERS

Katie Fields—This Jill-of-all-trades newly discovered twin sister is injured, and their honeymooning mother is missing. Can Katie reclaim her family before it's too late?

Nick Pierce—A widower whose three-year-old daughter is his sole priority. Can Katie convince him he's her mother's only hope?

Lily Pierce—A three-year-old enchantress whose mother died tragically. It doesn't take Katie long to realize why Nick will go to the ends of the earth to protect Lily.

Caroline Mays-Swope—Katie's missing mother. She's made some difficult decisions in her life. Have they now come back to haunt her?

Bill Thurman (aka Bill Swope)—Nick's father and Caroline's new husband. Trouble follows this man.

Helen Delaney—Nick's housekeeper and Lily's babysitter. She's sworn to do whatever it takes to keep Lily safe.

Frank Carson—This cop gone bad brags that he always gets his man. What else is he searching for?

Benito Mutzi—A mob boss who wants back what was once his. He isn't finicky about how he goes about it.

Doc—An old army buddy of Nick's. It helps to know a doctor who won't ask tricky questions about gunshot wounds.

FBI agent Loni Boone—Is she as good as her word or does she have her own agenda?

Tess Mays—Katie's twin sister, injured while helping Katie, depending now on Katie to help her.

Ryan Hill—The Oregon cop who loves Tess.

Prologue

She awoke in the dark, head throbbing, throat dry. For a second, she didn't have the slightest idea where she was or what had happened to her.

First things first. Get to your feet. Find out where you are.

Struggling to her knees, she reached forward until her hands touched a rough, damp dirt wall. Leveraging her body, she attempted to stand. Her head hit the ceiling while she was still crouching and she cried out, her voice a muffled squeak. Wherever she was, there was no standing room and she sank back down to the dirt floor, a geyser of hopelessness welling up inside her chest.

Into the cold, dank air she whispered, "My name is Caroline. I have a daughter named Tess."

This last thought made her wince.

Thoughts of her beloved Tess always made her wince. Not because of Tess herself, but because of Katie, frozen forever in her mind as a six-month-old baby, born in the spring when the roses bloomed…

Flowers! White roses. Yellow freesias.

Of course…a wedding…her wedding…

Bill!

Visions of men with masks, men with guns. Bill crumpled on the motel floor…

Tears filled her eyes and rolled down her cheeks as the past few days came back in total clarity.

Bill.

Where was Bill?

Chapter One

Nick Pierce stood on the tarmac gazing upward, though he knew from experience the high mountain air of Frostbite, Alaska, meant he'd hear the single-engine plane before he actually saw it.

He was anxious to get this over with. He was anxious to get back home. There was nothing he could tell the woman flying out of her way to talk to him. He would have made that clear when she called, but like an ostrich hiding its head in the sand, he'd figured if he ignored her she'd go away, and he'd never actually taken one of her calls himself.

It hadn't worked. Hell, that approach to problems never worked, but he always seemed compelled to give it a try anyway.

To top it off, the weather was changing. He could feel the cold bite of an approaching storm on his face, sweeping over the inlet, up the Panhandle, bringing snow and ice. Winter days were short this far north and at two-thirty in the afternoon, there was only about an hour of daylight left. Oh, face it—he was sorely tempted to drive away and forgo the meeting before he got stuck at the airport.

And then he heard a drone overhead and realized the time to leave had come and gone. A few minutes later, Toby Macleod's aqua DeHavilland Otter came to a stop a few yards away from Nick's four-wheel-drive truck, the wheel skis making slide marks in the accumulating snow. Nick stamped his feet to get his circulation moving, waiting for Toby to turn off the big turbo engine, then walked around to the far side of the plane, waving at Toby as he did so.

The sole passenger making the long climb out of the plane was bundled up to her ears in black boots, jeans and an olive-green parka, her head wrapped securely in a pale blue wool scarf. When she looked around to survey her surroundings, flaming red tendrils escaped the folds of wool, snapping like scarlet ribbons against the increasingly white environment. Reaching up and taking her ungloved hand, he helped her step down.

She stumbled as her right foot touched the ground, immediately straightening herself. Her head barely came level with his shoulder. She struck him as small, delicate, and out of place as she shoved her hands in her pockets and shivered.

"You're Nicolas Pierce," she said through clattering teeth, looking up at him with eyes as deep and blue as a fjord. She was extremely pretty and extremely young, at least to his world-weary eyes. He'd be thirty-eight in a few months and this woman looked about eighteen, though he guessed she was actually in her early twenties.

Taking her arm, he ushered her around the plane toward his truck.

"Call me Nick," he said, the weather clock ticking in his head. "And you're Tess Mays," he added.

He felt her flinch through her padded coat. "No, my name is Katie Fields."

"I don't understand," he snapped, suddenly suspicious. Helen, his housekeeper, had said his father's new stepdaughter had called a few times, the last to announce the fact she was on her way. The stepdaughter's name was Tess. He turned to look down at the woman beside him. "Who?" he snapped.

"Katie Fields. I'm Tess's sister." She glanced up for a second, her breath a cloud of icy vapor, a few sparkling ice crystals sticking to her cheeks and brow.

"I don't understand," he repeated, but he resumed ushering her forward as she appeared about ready to freeze in place. The limp grew more pronounced as she hurried beside him.

"It's a little complicated," she told him as he opened the truck door for her, struggling for a second as the heavy metal met the resistance of the quickening wind.

Gripping her shoulders, he leaned down to talk close to her ear so she could hear him. "It's too cold to stand around discussing things. Stay inside where it's warm while I talk to Toby. I'll be right back."

With his help, she made the high step up into the cab of his truck, hunkering down in the leather seat with a sigh of relief, covering her lower face with her bare hands, breathing into them in an effort to defrost her nose and lips and fingers, too. He'd done the same thing a million times since relocating here from southern California.

"Turn up the heater," he told her as the

wind finally won the tug-of-war with the door and slammed it back into place. He nodded reassuringly through the window at her alarmed expression, then went back to the plane.

At his approach, Toby opened a little window by the pilot's seat and poked his face cautiously through. Snowflakes immediately stuck to his beard and bushy red eyebrows.

"Hey, Nick," Toby called. "How's Lily?"

"Growing like a weed. How about Chris?"

"Two more weeks before the baby comes. She's about ready to explode." He grinned. Apparently, the thought of becoming a father for the fifth time pleased him. "Say, the weather is deteriorating quick," Toby added. "I've got medicine aboard for the Lambert woman in Skie. I've got to get it to her, which means I have to be able to take off from here. You've got five minutes with the lady, tops."

"It won't take even that long," Nick said.

He retraced his steps to the truck and climbed aboard, struggling with the door again.

Now he faced Katie Fields, who had warmed to the point that she'd unwrapped her hair and unzipped her parka. He could have saved her the trouble. Five minutes wasn't long enough for anyone to get cozy.

As he pulled off his gloves, he took a good look at her face, trying to see something of her mother in her, but he'd never actually met the woman, just seen a wedding photograph sent north by Tess Mays. As he'd torn it in half the moment he figured out what it was, there was nothing left but a vague impression of a middle-aged woman with wispy, graying blond hair.

There was nothing, however, wispy about her daughter. Katie Fields might be small, but passion burned in her eyes like twin fireballs. Her red hair heightened this perception. Her golden eyebrows suggested she was actually a natural blonde, like Patricia, and with the thought of his late wife, his heart seized for an interminable moment.

"Like I said, I'm Tess's sister," Katie said, jerking him back to the present. "She didn't know about me until recently—"

He shook his head as he pulled off his black wool cap. Straight strands of sandy hair fell into his eyes and he brushed them out of the way. "We don't have time for details," he told her. "You've made this trip for nothing and I'm sorry about that, but I don't have anything to tell you. If I'd taken your call I could have saved you the expense of this trip."

"But you were never around to take the call," she said, and he got the distinct impression she knew perfectly well that he'd avoided this discussion like the plague. He shrugged.

"Your father—"

"As far as I'm concerned," he interrupted, "my *father* was the perfectly ordinary man who married my mother when I was eight years old. His name was Jim Pierce. He adopted me and undertook the task of raising me. He owned a shoe store in San Diego. He played golf and told bad jokes. He died ten years ago. He was a great guy and I still miss him."

She looked confused. Stuttering, she muttered, "But I thought…Tess said…your father…"

"Your mother's new husband is my biological father. I'm sorry your family got mixed up with him. But again, I haven't seen the man in over two years and if my luck holds, I'll never see Bill Thurman again."

"My mother married a man named Bill Swope."

"Seems as though Dad got himself a brand-new name."

"Why would he do that?"

More memories of Patricia invaded his head, but this time her own blood soaked her blond hair. Looking over Katie's shoulder, Nick pulled on his gloves. "Toby is gesturing like crazy, the weather is about to close in, you have a plane to catch," he said in a clipped voice.

Avoiding her gaze, he tugged on his hat and pushed open the door. The weather had further deteriorated in the few short minutes he'd been inside and the blast of cold air streaming into the truck had his visitor shivering again. He darted around and opened her door, anxious to get this woman into Toby's plane before it was too late. She sat in the seat looking down at him, her scarf still in her lap, her pretty face puzzled.

"Come on," he said, reaching up for her. Time was up.

She bit her bottom lip, then shook her head. "No."

The wind was howling; he must have heard her wrong. He glanced at the plane. Toby had rubbed a clear space on the inside of the windshield and could be seen holding up one finger.

"I'm not leaving," she yelled. "You have to help me."

"I told you—"

"Listen," she said, her voice still loud but her tone somber. "I get it. You don't like your bio dad. I couldn't care less what your problem with him is, all I know is he's disappeared with my mother, a woman I haven't seen since I was a few months old. My sister is lying in a hospital with a gunshot wound, worrying herself sick. My mother and your father never showed up in Seattle where they had reservations at a downtown hotel. I'm going to find our mother and take her to my sister, and if that means I have to stay in this frozen wasteland till the blasted daises pop through the snow, then so be it."

He stared at her with disbelieving eyes. She couldn't be serious. On the other hand, there was something about the stubborn tilt of her chin that suggested otherwise and it came to him with a jolt: Katie Fields wasn't bluffing. Or budging.

He slammed her door and approached the

DeHavilland, gesturing with his arm for Toby to take off. Toby disappeared for a moment and then opened the door and threw out a small brown suitcase that landed with a thud. After Nick retrieved the bag, he stood there in the freezing snow as Toby started the engine and taxied down the runway, gaining momentum, lifting to the sky and almost instantly disappearing. Being a pilot himself, he knew Toby would make it to Skie within an hour, and that Skie's weather was never as bad as Frostbite's.

Then he turned to look back at his truck and the woman sitting inside.

He'd have to take her home with him.

As he labored through the gathering snow, Katie Fields's suitcase clenched under his arm, Nick swore at his father, wherever he was, and at the woman trusting enough to fall for his lies and marry him.

Bill Swope?

What was going on? Just exactly what had his father roped Katie Fields's mother into?

Hopefully she wouldn't pay for her naiveté with her life.

Chapter Two

Judging distances in the blizzard surrounding the truck was almost impossible for Katie, though there did seem to be some distant mountains looming ahead. She'd spent her life on the Oregon coast, where it seldom snowed; this experience was like being immersed in one of those bleak Christmas cards that are supposed to look cheery.

No one could accuse Nick Pierce, however, of looking cheery.

She wrapped her cold hands in the folds of her scarf and wished she'd thought to swallow a couple of aspirin before debarking the plane. The coma she'd recently suffered still left her with headaches, and her injured leg throbbed despite the fact the doctor said it was mending well.

She sneaked a peek at Nick, who gripped the steering wheel with both hands, brow furrowed in concentration as he expertly handled the big truck. She could feel tension emanating from him like the warm blasts shooting out of the heater. She doubted his stress had anything to do with the driving and everything to do with her presence in his life.

Truth was, she was almost as perplexed by her behavior as he seemed to be. Sure, she was tenacious. Anyone who knew her knew that. But she was also driving in a snowstorm with a stranger. Once back in the truck, he'd announced she had no choice but to accompany him and he was headed home before he got snowed in at the airport. He didn't equivocate or wait for her permission. It was as though she'd abandoned all free will the moment she let the plane leave the ground without her, and though she understood now that was exactly what she'd done, it didn't make swallowing it less alarming.

Still, she'd do it again in a flash. This man knew things about his biological father that she needed to know, and one way or another, she was determined to worm them out of him.

She couldn't explain why she was so sure something was wrong; like she'd told Nick, she hadn't actually seen her mother in twenty-six-and-a-half years. Maybe it was her newly discovered twin sister's certainty that their mother was in danger that had communicated itself to Katie, planted itself deep in her subconscious, making Tess's distress as real as her own. After all, Tess had grown up with their mother and knew the woman as well as Katie had known their father.

That thought jolted her. Her father had led a secret life that had damn near gotten both his daughters killed. Known him? How well does a child *really* know a parent? How much is an illusion?

But she did know, or was getting to know, Tess. She could sense her sister's moods and thoughts in a mysterious way that felt totally natural. She knew Tess didn't understand this dimension of their relationship. They'd talked as long and as much as Tess's precarious condition allowed before Katie flew north, and Tess admitted she'd never had an inkling she wasn't an only child before the call that Katie had been injured came from the New Harbor police.

On the other hand, Katie had always felt half-complete. She'd spent her life looking for something. Now she realized she'd been looking for *someone*. She'd been looking for Tess. She took her new cell phone out of her pocket and punched it on. The old one had been seized by the Oregon police as evidence.

No signal.

"We're almost there," Nick said, turning off what appeared to be a main highway though they'd not met a single car for a mile or two, since the buildings had stopped and Katie had all but given up hope Nick lived in the middle of a nice, bustling community. She peered through the window but all she saw were pristine white flakes, illuminated by the headlights and falling steadily all around them.

"I'll take your word for it," she said, re-pocketing the useless phone and turning in her seat to look at him. He appeared to be in his mid-thirties, a tall man who seemed strong and healthy. He had a way of walking that suggested that beneath all those layers of clothes there was an extremely fit man who knew exactly where he was going and where he'd been, as though he plotted and planned his every move and hadn't made a spontaneous decision in his whole life.

His self-confidence suddenly goaded her

into a small explosion. "Why do you hate your biological father so much?" she demanded. "What do you think he's done with my mother? Is he dangerous? Should I call the FBI?"

He deflected her outburst with a single question. "Haven't you contacted the police already?"

"Sure we contacted them. First my sister's fiancé called, then I did. They said to give her a while, that a middle-aged woman on her honeymoon might choose *not* to stay in touch. The fact their hotel reservation was canceled tells the police they just changed their mind about their destination."

"They canceled the reservation?"

She said, "Don't dodge my question. Why is your father so...I don't know, so loathsome to you? Do you think he purposely hurt my mother?"

Nick glanced at her briefly before turning back to study the road. In that glance, Katie felt the full impact of his eyes. They were as green as palm trees, and thickly lashed, and why she hadn't been knocked overboard long before this by the sheer clarity and intensity of his gaze made her wonder if her libido had frozen along with her fingers and nose.

He had a very strong profile, all clean lines and determined thrust of chin, a man to be reckoned with. Maybe a man who figured everyone who wasn't with him was against him.

She'd have to make sure she got him on her side. No trouble, right? She was a people person, a bartender for years, a Jill of all trades.

Did she have dreams? Of course. What would life be like without dreams? But she'd learned to put her dreams on a back burner. Money was, and had always been, tight and she'd kept her dreams close to her heart, guarding them against the reality of barely making ends meet. What little she had saved she'd used up financing the search for the truth concerning her father's death. She wouldn't have been able to afford this trip, for instance, if her veterinarian sister hadn't put it on her credit card.

Katie couldn't think about her father right now. It was still too painful. She'd get Nick to come around. She had to. All she needed was time, and judging from the weather, time was just what she had working on her side.

What about her mother? Did Caroline have time or was it already too late?

"Maybe we could share what information we have," she said, attempting to calm herself down. The truck bounced through a gulley and she gritted her teeth as her leg throbbed anew.

"Let's just get home first," he said, driving over a small bridge.

At last the dark shadows of the mountains grew closer and the contours of a log house, glowing with light, smoke rising from its chimney, caught her attention. It was built on the edge of a small, iced-over lake complete with a short pier. A light mounted high on a pole beside the pier illuminated the falling snow. There were also a number of smaller cabins clustered near the main house, as well as a long building set off by itself. Every structure boasted steeply pitched green metal roofs, set in among a million trees, a setting so peaceful it should have calmed Katie's nerves.

But in fact, the beauty and serenity just made her more antsy. What could they possibly get done out here? She'd jumped out of a frying pan into a fire—or out of an ice chest into a freezer—pick a metaphor, any one would do. And it was her own damn, impulsive fault.

"We're here," Nick said, slowing the truck.

"You own all this?"

"Yes."

"It's huge."

"It was built by a painter back in 1950. He used to open it up in the summer for aspiring artists with enough cash to fly in and spend several weeks under his tutelage. I bought it from him four or five years ago."

"Are you an artist too?" she asked.

He replied immediately. "No. My wife was."

"Your wife—"

He stilled her with a swift, intense green glance. "She died two years ago," he said, his voice as bleak as his expression.

"I'm sorry."

"So am I." He pressed a button on the visor above his head and the door to a large garage rolled up and out of the way. Nick pulled inside, his headlights illuminating a couple of snowmobiles and a blue van. A door opposite suggested covered passage to the house. The door was closing and Nick was out of the truck before Katie could untangle her hands from her scarf. He flipped on an overhead light and the details of winter equipment like snowblowers, boots, sleds and snowshoes came into sharp focus.

He opened her door and once again she faced the long step down from the truck. Her leg ached at the prospect. "Are there other people here now?" Katie asked hopefully as she slid from her seat. Nick seemed to be prepared for her ungainly exit and caught her in a grip as solid as granite.

"Not in the winter. This time of year it's just me and Helen, my housekeeper. And Lily, of course."

"Nick, please talk to me about your father," she said, gazing up into his eyes, imploring him to stop evading her questions. "Time is passing and my mother is missing."

"I know," he said. "But there's a storm coming and no one will be going anywhere for a while. We almost always lose phone service in weather like this. In short, your problem will keep. I want to see if Lily is still awake."

"Who's Lily?"

"My daughter." He reached past her and retrieved her suitcase, then opened the connecting door to what appeared to be an enclosed porch. A row of hooks held outerwear, a tray underneath caught the drips as snow melted. Baskets lined up on a shelf were filled with mittens, gloves and stocking caps. Nick pulled off his hat and tossed it into a basket; his gloves followed a second later. He unzipped his coat and took it off, carefully hanging it on an empty hook next to a pale yellow coat with a fur collar that was so tiny it had to belong to a child.

Katie took off her own coat and immediately missed its warm, cozy lining even though she wore a thick sweater underneath. Nick took it from her and hung it on a hook before parking himself on a bench and unlacing his boots.

"Are your feet wet?" he asked Katie. He pointed at her suitcase. "Do you have something dry and warm in there or do you need to borrow slippers?"

He was wearing a green flannel shirt that stretched across his shoulders as he moved. He was built splendidly, Katie saw, broad at the shoulder, narrow through the hips, tall and straight, sent from central casting to play the role of handsome, defensive, sexy recluse.

But he was real. Those eyes, that tenderness in his voice when his daughter's name passed his lips, his single-minded straight-as-an-arrow determination to do things his own way in his own time—all man, all real and, probably, all obstacle.

"My feet are fine," she said, looking down at her own boots. She'd been traveling the better part of two days to get here. Flights from Oregon to Washington, then on to Anchorage, Alaska. Then the bush-pilot flight to Frostbite. Now she was out here in the middle of nowhere, trying to get a man to talk, a man who obviously didn't want to talk, and just how was she supposed to ever get home again?

And what about her mother?

As she folded her head scarf and straightened the gray wool sweater she wore over a light blue turtleneck shirt, she admitted that her head pounded, her leg ached, she was cold and hungry and frustrated. "Nick—" she said impatiently.

Once again he cut her off, this time by standing abruptly. He'd slipped on a pair of dry loafers. As he opened the door leading into the house, she picked up her suitcase and followed. What choice did she have?

Aromas of roasting meat and vegetables perfumed the room they entered, a kitchen full of rough wood beams and rich dark tiles. Some kind of fruit pie—apple?—sat cooling on a wooden board. Katie's stomach growled.

"Mr. Nick," a woman said, looking up from the sink where she peeled potatoes. She appeared to be in her late fifties, Katie guessed, with long black hair gathered into a low-riding ponytail, silver threads running throughout. She was short and comfortable looking, her skin winter-white, her dark eyes liquid in the subdued light.

"I thought maybe you got stuck at the airport…" the woman began, her voice trailing off as Katie stepped from behind Nick.

The friendly smile wavered.

Katie was blasted with a fresh wave of alarm. Was everyone in Frostbite suspicious of outsiders?

Nick said, "Helen, this is Katie Fields, the woman I went to meet today. Katie, Helen Delaney, the woman who runs things around here."

Helen raked Katie over with narrowed eyes but addressed her comments to Nick. "I thought you were meeting your father's stepdaughter. The one who called here. Theresa Mays."

"Katie is apparently my…father's…other stepdaughter," Nick said.

"I'm the one who called you the last time," Katie explained, sticking out her free hand. "I'm sorry for the confusion."

Helen dried her hand on her apron and took Katie's hand, her gaze averted as she mumbled a polite greeting. Katie said the first thing that popped to her mind. "That pie looks delicious."

"Apple rhubarb," Helen said. "Mr. Nick's favorite." She turned her attention back to Nick and added, "I didn't know you were bringing anyone back to the house. I didn't expect company."

Nick said, "The weather turned. Toby had to get some medicine to Skie." He ran a hand through his dark blond hair before looking at Katie. "Well, you're here now and, by the looks of the weather, you aren't going anywhere for a couple of days. I'll show you to a guest room in a few moments, but first I need to look in on my daughter."

"I gave her an early dinner and put her to bed," Helen said, darting Katie a surreptitious glance. Katie felt distinctly uncomfortable. Helen had seemed cordial enough on the phone, so why the cool welcome? And did Nick have to talk to her as it she was an intruder?

Whoa, reality check. You forced yourself on both of them, an inner voice whispered. *No one asked you to come, you just refused to leave.*

She rubbed her forehead. She'd packed doctor-prescribed painkillers in her suitcase and the temptation to down half a bottle and sleep the storm out was amazingly strong but she knew she'd settle for a couple of aspirin instead. She needed to stay clearheaded and focused.

"I'll be right back," Nick said, glancing down at her.

She grabbed his arm as he turned and felt his muscles tense beneath her grasp. "You have to tell me about your father," she said vehemently. "I need to understand what's going on. I have to find my mother. I know you think I'm overreacting—"

He stared at her hand. For a second, she expected him to bat it away, but then he did something even worse. Laying his hand gently over the top of hers he said, "No, I don't think you're overreacting."

"So you *do* think she's in danger."

"If she married my father, I'd be willing to bet on it," he told her, his eyes intense and serious. "I'm sorry."

Chapter Three

Nick loved this time of day the best.

Lily, cheeks rosy, fair hair glistening in the subdued bedside light, smelling of soap, eyes sleepy but resolute, small arms anxious to wrap around his neck, voice soft and sweet as she asked him to read her a story.

His Lily, a small carbon copy of her mother except for the color of her eyes, which mirrored his own, and the stubborn streak she'd picked up from his side of the family, as well. Patricia had called Lily the perfect combination of the two of them, and they had spent hours musing over who their future children would look like, be like.

Fate had snatched away the possibility of future children. Fate in the form of his father.

He read Lily a story about a bird that lived on top of a palm tree on the island of Maui. As Lily had been born right here in Frostbite and hadn't left the state of Alaska once in her three years, he often wondered how she could relate to palm trees and grass skirts, green and yellow birds and brilliant flowers. When she was old enough, he'd recently decided, he'd take her to Hawaii and show her all the things the book promised, from luaus to warm ocean water.

For now, he finished the story by gently tickling her, which was part of the ritual, and then he kissed her warm forehead and held her hand as she drifted off to sleep.

And tried not to think about the redheaded problem in his kitchen.

The wind had come up while he'd been busy with Lily, and he returned to the kitchen to find the lights flickering and Helen absent. He could hear naked limbs scratching against the tin roof and the sound of an unclosed gate from out near the pier.

Had Helen been walking out there earlier today?

After stoking the living-room fireplace, he lit a couple of kerosene lanterns in anticipation of losing the lights. His was the last house connected to Frostbite's power lines and the first to lose electricity during bad weather. He'd start the generator if it looked like the electricity loss was going to go beyond a few hours.

He found Katie in the kitchen standing at the sink, draining a pot, steam billowing around her flushed face. She looked over her shoulder as he came into the room.

"Where's Helen?" he said.

"She showed me which bedroom to take then pleaded a headache," Katie said, turning to face him. She held a pot of boiled potatoes in one hand and the masher in the other. "How do you feel about kitchen duties?"

"No problem," he said, still puzzling over Helen's odd behavior. "She just left?"

"She just left." Katie leaned against the counter as he retrieved butter and milk from the refrigerator and added, "Frankly, I don't think she likes me."

He crashed the masher into the pot. He found Katie's tendency to blurt out exactly what was on her mind a little disconcerting.

"She's choosy," he said.

Katie laughed. "Thanks a lot."

"Don't take me wrong," he said, adding butter and seasonings to the pot. "Your coming to Frostbite is a reminder of a lot of things Helen would like to forget, all revolving around my dear old dad. Your coming into this house is like rubbing salt in an old wound."

"I've never even met your father!"

"Doesn't matter," he said.

"For heaven's sake. How about you? You'd like to forget a lot of things about your father, too, right?"

"Like the fact he ever existed? Yeah, you're right," he said, whipping in the milk, his mind closing against the pain Katie's probing caused. "I would."

Except for the sound of the wind howling outside, dinner was a more or less silent affair. Katie swirled mashed potatoes into her gravy, casting him occasional wary glances as though trying to gauge if she could trust him.

The answer was yes. And no.

It all depended.

She could trust him to put up with her until he could get rid of her, to try to answer a few questions, but she couldn't trust him to spring into action and solve all her problems. Since Patricia's death, he had one blinding obligation and that was his daughter. Period.

Besides, his action days were behind him,

lost now in the haze of his Army Ranger years, his stealth and manual-combat skills as rusty as his aim though he still maintained a closetful of weapons. Hell, every man, woman and child in Frostbite, Alaska, knew how to shoot a gun. It went with the territory.

All this justification made him uneasy, especially when he glanced at his dinner guest and met her troubled blue gaze. If her mother was half as innocent as her daughter, the poor woman was in for a lot of trouble.

Though he tried to dissuade her, Katie helped him clear the table and wash the dishes. He wasn't crazy about standing so close to her in the kitchen. The room had always been the warm, comforting heart of the house. Katie brought a level of tension with her that ruined this ambience and he resented her intrusion. The thought flitted through his mind that things were soon going to go from bad to worse. His level of uneasiness began to creep up off the charts.

The electricity went out as he put the last plate on the open shelf.

He stacked more wood on the fire and lit another lantern, which he used to go check on Lily who was sound asleep. He replaced her kicked-off covers. As he walked back down the dark hallway, he noticed a light on under the door of Helen's room.

He raised his hand to knock to make sure she was okay, to try to cajole her back into the kitchen so she could get herself something to eat. Before his knuckles touched the wood, the door swung open.

Helen faced him, carrying a small backpack in her hand. She'd changed into her snow clothes—thermal, watertight overalls and a blue jacket with a hood. A pair of heavily insulated gloves dangled around her neck on a tether. Her feet were clad in thick socks, awaiting boots, he supposed.

He said, "Helen?"

"I'm going to my sister's house," she said.

He stared at her a second. She'd been part of his household for years and to say her current behavior was out of character was like saying if an elephant took a hankering to sit down, he'd need more than one chair.

Nick shook his head.

"I can't stay here. I can't bear to hear talk about *him*. Why did *she* come here? She's going to make things worse—"

She stopped abruptly and met his gaze, her large dark eyes swimming in pain. He knew exactly what she was thinking, because he'd been thinking it himself. By coming to this house, Katie Fields had unintentionally brought the past alive. He said, "Is your sister expecting you?"

"None of the phones work."

"Damn, we lost the phone line already? I'm going to have to break down and get a cell phone one of these days."

"It doesn't mater. My sister will be home. I'm sorry, Mr. Nick, to abandon you—"

"I'll drive you—"

"The snow's too deep. Even if you got me there, you'd never get back. I'll take one of the snowmobiles."

"Helen—"

"It's not far. And you have Lily to watch."

She sidled past him and he made no move to stop her, but he didn't like her going off into a storm by herself. On the other hand, he couldn't take Lily out into this weather. Well, well, his visitor might come in handy after all. "Wait," he called, approaching Helen. He spoke fast and low. She shook her head, but he ignored her and went looking for Katie.

This time he found her in the living room, seated in a big red chair pulled up close to the fire, and for a second, his breath caught.

Firelight danced across her face, sparkled in her eyes, glistened in her hair. She sat forward, warming her hands, her trim body taut. She looked so bright and so alive she rivaled the fire itself.

He rubbed his eyes before entering the room and stood with his back to the fire, staring down at her.

"Is everything okay?" she asked.

"Yeah, fine." Reluctantly, he added, "I need a favor."

She immediately nodded. "Of course."

"Helen is taking a snowmobile into Frostbite to visit her sister. I'm not comfortable with her going out in this alone. Will you keep an eye on Lily while I give Helen a ride? It shouldn't take more than twenty or thirty minutes and Lily is sound asleep. I doubt she'll stir."

"Helen is leaving because of me, isn't she?"

"It's her choice. I won't be long."

Katie said, "I spent half my youth babysitting. I'd love to watch Lily."

Helen was sitting on the bench out on the porch, lacing up her boots. He put on his snow gear. In unison, they moved to the garage, where they both pulled on helmets.

Nick pushed the larger of the snowmobiles out the door. As he and Helen roared away from the house, he looked back once, reassured by the flickering of the lanterns visible through the falling snow, his home a comfortable island floating on mounds of pristine white.

KATIE WATCHED the retreating lights of the snowmobile disappear, with her hands clenched into fists at her side.

It all came down to time.

Time for stories read to a child, time for Helen to get sulky and distant, to require aid, to retreat.

Time to eat and wash dishes, time to build fires and light lanterns, time for everything and everyone except her mother, the one person to whom every second might mean the difference between life and death.

What was going on? Why was it so hard to get an answer to anything in this house?

She turned away from the window in a huff, frustration demanding movement, movement all but impossible unless it was contained within the log structure. She stomped down the hall until she found an open door with a soft light coming from within. An oversize window covered with lacy curtains took up half of one wall. The bed was positioned in such a way that a person could look outside while lying down. The view must be gorgeous when it was actually possible to see outside.

Nick had left a lantern burning on his daughter's dresser; its flickering light cast dancing shadows against the walls, but it also bathed a sleeping child's face. Katie covered her mouth with her hand and stared.

Lily Pierce was an angel on earth. Fine blond hair, long dark lashes, rosebud mouth, rounded cheeks…the whole nine yards. She was the treasure inside the castle, the princess inside the steeple, and all of a sudden, Nick's fierce determination to see to her needs at any cost made a little more sense.

Katie backed quietly out into the hall, returning to the living room, sitting back down in the red chair, holding her hands toward the fire not so much because she was cold as because the sounds of the storm made her feel cold.

And alone.

Wind rustled in the trees, whistled in the eaves, banged things together, blew snow against the windows. The interior of the house was warm and welcoming in the way a port in a storm always is, but despite the reassuringly thick walls and the beautiful slumbering child a few steps away, the underlying tensions between Nick and herself, to say nothing of Helen's abrupt departure, eroded the comfort level, letting the cold seep between the logs of polite construction.

Katie settled back in the chair, closing her eyes. Her headache had disappeared with the ingestion of Helen's excellent meal, but her leg still throbbed and she knew fatigue fueled her distress. For once she was glad Tess couldn't pick up any telepathic vibes, because the maelstrom inside Katie's head wouldn't do anyone any good, especially not Tess. Tess needed to put her energy into healing, not worrying.

Katie should have gotten back on that blasted plane. She'd been here for three hours and nothing had happened except she'd eaten dinner and made an enemy. Why was Helen so determined not to give her a chance?

She opened her eyes and surveyed the surrounding room. The rock fireplace took up most of one wall. A wooden door about two feet square led to a supply of firewood—she'd checked. The wide hearth was two feet off the ground with a few cushions tossed atop, making extra seating. One photo sat on the mantel, framed in heavy wood. A blond woman holding a baby. Nick's late wife, no doubt, Lily as an infant. The other walls, logs chinked with what appeared to be cement, were covered with watercolors, beautiful paintings of hillsides and wild-flowers, snowy peaks and exotic animals. The furniture was big and comfortable, ta-bletops cluttered with toys and books and camera equipment. Because of the log con-struction, the windows were deep and dark—

A face suddenly appeared in one of the front windows. Gasping, Katie shot to her feet. A man's face but not Nick's. Fuller, unshaved, dark eyes furtive.

And then it was gone—poof!—as though it had never been there.

Katie stood stock-still for several moments, her mind racing. Was the door locked? Were all the doors locked? She moved quickly to the front door and found a chain in place. She started to undo it, to open the door, to peer outside and call out, but her hand stilled at the last moment and she dropped it, leaning back against the door, listening, waiting.

Nothing. No knock. The silence was ominous.

She went through the kitchen to the back door. It, too, was locked. She didn't know if there were other doors. Spying the phone on the wall, she plucked off the receiver, ready to call 911 and probably make a fool of herself. The line was dead. She dug her cell phone from her pocket. The screen lit at her touch. Still no signal.

She was alone. Well, except for the slumbering child down the hall.

Katie retraced her steps to the living room and the fireplace, sitting back on her red chair, staring toward the window, a black portal buffeted now and again by nothing more sinister than a snow flurry.

"Who are you?" a high-pitched voice said from her elbow.

For the second time that night, Katie gasped as her heart did a little stop-and-start thing in her chest. Lily Pierce stood nearby in pink footy pajamas, tousled fair hair a halo around her head, round cheeks blooming with pink. She held a gray stuffed bunny by one ear.

Hoping the child wouldn't burst into tears or run from the room, Katie said, "My name is Katie."

"Where's Helen? Where's Daddy?"

"Daddy took Helen to visit her sister—"

"Went to Auntie Joy's house?"

Sounded reasonable to Katie. She said, "I think so. Daddy will be back very soon. Did something wake you, sweetheart? Did you, uh, see someone?"

The child shook her head. She shuffled a little and Katie started to get up to follow her back to her room and tuck her into bed, but Lily came to stop right in front of Katie.

"You know 'bout the birdie in the palm tree?" she asked.

Katie said, "I don't think so."

"I tell you?"

Happy for the company, Katie patted her knee. "Okay."

The little girl climbed onto Katie's lap, squirming around until she fit comfortably, her head right under Katie's nose, her fine hair fluttering when Katie exhaled a breath. She presented a warm, sweet-smelling bundle, totally at ease, one dimpled hand clutching the bunny, the other hand laying idle on Katie's arm except for a single finger she used to stroke Katie's watchband.

The wind howled outside and rattled the door. A shiver ran up Katie's spine and she wrapped her arms around Lily. She wasn't sure what else to do. In fact, she was beginning to wonder if she'd imagined the man at the window.

"'Bout that birdie—" Lily whispered, launching into a story that Katie tried her best to understand. She could only catch every third word, however, so she nodded a lot and murmured appropriate remarks. She kept her eyes focused on the window, jerking every time a gust of wind made something outside bang or clatter. Her other senses were attuned to Lily. Her clean little-girl smell, her warm weight in Katie's arms, her soft voice.

Katie liked children—always had, though she'd been raised an only child with no younger cousins to play with. There had been the neighbor kids, though, younger than she, a veritable gold mine of babysitting money. This child took the cake, however. She was not only physically attractive, but she was charming and trusting and her eyes twinkled.

Katie hugged Lily tighter and, instead of resisting, the child relaxed. Her body grew heavier, the string of the story faded into words interspersed with yawns until there were no more words, just soft breathing and a heavy head on Katie's shoulder.

Katie knew she should carry the child off to her bed, but the temptation to hold her in front of the crackling fire was too great to resist. Besides, she didn't want to be alone. Where was Nick?

What she wanted was for him to come home and reassure her with something along the lines of: "That face in the window? Not to worry, that's old man Petrie, a harmless recluse. The old coot likes to wander around in snowstorms looking for aluminum cans." That would be great. She could handle old man Petrie…

Resting her cheek atop Lily's spun-gold hair and kissing her forehead, Katie closed her eyes, listening to the storm outside. Both the anxiety concerning the face at the window and worry about her mother's welfare took a back seat as exhaustion caught up with her, spinning her thoughts into ever-more-distant circles.

She must have fallen asleep, for the next

thing Katie knew, a door slammed her back to consciousness. Nick Pierce stood just inside the room, the expression on his face unfathomable.

"What are you doing with my daughter?" he said, striding across the room.

A sudden stab of guilt made Katie flinch. She should have put the little girl back in her bed, but honestly, was it really such a big deal?

Katie said, "I—"

He leaned over and picked Lily up, shifting her in his arms, his embrace of his sleeping child as tender as it was protective.

"What's your problem?" she snapped, her voice a sharp whisper. "Your child needed comforting and so I—"

"Lily is—"

"*Your* daughter. I got that. This place is a nuthouse! How she turned out so endearing—"

"No one asked you to come here," he said, his expression so intense it would probably start a blaze if directed on one spot long enough.

"You're right," she said, standing. "And trust me, as soon as I can figure out a way to leave, I'll be out of your hair. You don't know anything about your father, do you? I bet you don't know anything about anyone, especially not yourself!"

"What the hell does that mean?" He kept his voice as low in volume as Katie did.

She glowered at him in response.

"I'm going to put Lily back in her bed. You stay here."

As though she had anywhere else to go!

Chapter Four

Nick tucked Lily into her bed, kissed her cheek and closed the door, leaving it open just a crack in case she called out. Then he stood in the hall and ran his hand through his hair.

That blasted woman! Coming into his house, scaring away his housekeeper, waking his kid, acting as though she owned the place, as though she had rights, as though she was an invited guest and not an interloper and a troublemaker and a major pain in the neck.

He had to get rid of her.

Oh, hell, he knew in the back of his mind that Lily sometimes woke up during storms and wandered out to see if anything interesting was going on without her. He should be grateful that Katie was there to comfort his baby, that Lily had felt comfortable enough to go to her, to sit on her lap, to fall asleep in her arms, but he wasn't grateful. He didn't know for sure what he felt, but it wasn't gratitude.

Taking a deep breath, he went back to the living room. Katie was still in the red chair. She looked up when he entered. "Your phone is dead," she said.

"I know. I should have told you it went down early in the storm. Listen, what do you want to know?" he asked, claiming a matching chair to the left of hers. It was time to get this over with.

"There's nothing you can tell me," she said without looking at him. There were dark circles beneath her eyes, and snippets of things she'd said about herself over the past few hours suddenly came back to him. She hadn't known her mother until recently? Her sister was in the hospital with a gunshot wound? And her limp. Why did she limp?

"Listen, let's start over again," he said.

She darted him a quick glance. "What's the point? You resent my being here. You're right, I foisted myself on you and your family. I don't know what I was thinking. I've made everything worse instead of better and now I'm stuck."

He chuckled. "You're pretty good," he said.

This earned him a longer look. "What do you mean?"

"Anger hasn't worked. Buttering me up with a poignant little vignette featuring my kid didn't do it. Now you're going to try humility."

He expected her to jump to her feet and strike out at him. Face it, it was the reaction he hoped for. Caring feelings toward this woman were impossible to entertain. She was trouble. Or to be more fair, she would bring trouble to his life and his family if given half a chance, so reason said push her far away using any method available.

He couldn't throw her out of the house, because she'd freeze to death. With the county roads in their current snowed-in condition and with no one to watch Lily, he couldn't even drive her back into Frostbite's lone hotel though, now that he thought of it, why hadn't he deposited her there instead of bringing her out here? He couldn't call her a cab or send her off on a snowmobile. Physically, he was stuck with Katie Fields, so the only method to get rid of her was to anger her beyond reason so she'd stalk off to the guest room and leave him in peace.

But she didn't jump up or turn nasty. "You really hate your father, don't you?"

He stared right into her blue eyes and smiled. "I really do."

She sighed. "First things first. Did you stand outside and look through that window over there a few minutes ago? Fifteen maybe, a half hour tops?"

"Absolutely not," he said quickly.

"I didn't think so."

"You saw someone?"

"Yes. He looked right through the window but by the time I blinked he was gone. Then Lily showed up so I kept her in here with me. I'd like to say it was for her sake, but truthfully, I just didn't want to be alone and she was so damn sweet and trusting—"

He held up a conciliatory hand. "I've fallen under her spell a time or two myself. Let's get back to the man at the window. What did he look like?"

"He had dark eyes and a haggard, unshaven look. That's all I could see. I think he was wearing a hood of some kind. He looked—intense, I guess. I went over to the door to check the chain and listen, but I couldn't hear anything."

Nick had walked to the door as Katie

spoke. She was right behind him. Taking a lantern from the table, he unhooked the chain and pulled open the door, letting in a blast of cold air and a few snowflakes. He shone the light out into the dark, cold night.

It was still snowing. Four or five new inches had accumulated on the porch railing. The grounds were blanketed in white, broken by the tall shapes of waving trees and long lines of fences all obscured by the storm. The eight guest cabins hovered off to the left, dark and silent and empty.

"Tell me where you saw him," he said, gesturing for Katie to join him on the porch.

She stepped outside, shivering, hugging herself. "The second window on the right," she said through chattering teeth. The covered porch stopped shy of the window a foot or so and they stood at the edge, looking down into the snow below the window, searching for some sign a man had walked to the window, had stood below it and looked inside.

There was nothing to be seen, however. The area was littered with rocks and the branches of dormant plants that formed natural pockets and rifts. If someone had created footprints that evening, it was already too late to tell.

Nick peered through the snow. From what he could see, everything looked about the same as usual.

"Are you sure you saw someone?" he said.

She looked up at him, preoccupied. "I thought I did. Maybe the storm spooked me."

"Let's go back inside."

He closed the door behind them, securing it once again with the chain. Katie immediately moved toward the fire, standing as close to the blaze as she could.

Nick didn't know what to make of Katie's story. The nearest neighbor was over a mile away and they were off in Florida for the winter. It was another mile to the Booths' place and then another half mile to the Stewart cabin.

Katie struck him as a woman with a very active imagination. He could see no covert reason for her to make up such a story, so undoubtedly she'd seen something, just not a man. Snow, a branch blowing by, a shadow. Trying to get things back on an even keel, he said, "Tell me a little more about you and your sister and why you're so sure there's a problem with your mother and my father."

She moved back to her chair, settling

herself on the edge of the cushion, hands folded in her lap. "As you know, my mother married your father after knowing him only three weeks. My sister assures me this was very out of character for her. Was it out of character for him, too?"

"How would I know?"

"Nick, please, try."

"Let me give you a little background," he said warily. "My very young mother married an alcoholic. She stuck with him for several years until she developed breast cancer. He took off like a shot never to be seen again, well at least not for umpteen years. Mom got better, married the shoe salesman, raised me. Let's see. I went into the Army. Fought in the Gulf War. Came home, stepdad died. I married Patricia, moved to Alaska, had Lily. Dad came for a heartwarming reunion, I turned him away, Patricia welcomed him with open arms. She died, he took off again—noticing a pattern?"

"So if something has happened to my mother—"

"He probably ran out and left her high-and-dry. Like I said, it wouldn't be the first time."

He was immediately sorry he said it.

Katie's pretty face literally collapsed as tears rolled down her cheeks. He stared into her huge blurry eyes for a second, not sure what to do, hoping she'd pull herself together, but if anything, the tears got worse. He got up from his chair and handed her the tissue box. Within a few moments, Katie dabbed at her eyes and took a few deep breaths. He poured them both a stiff brandy, handed her a snifter and sat back down, twirling the amber liquid in his glass, wishing he could float away on its fumes.

"Listen, Katie, I'm sorry," he said at last. "I haven't been very tactful. I'm rusty, I guess. Until tonight, Helen pretty much took care of herself, and Lily is still in the kiss-it-and-make-it-better stage. Everything just seems to be suddenly falling apart."

"And you blame me," she said.

True, but this time he stayed quiet.

Katie took a sip of the liquor and set the glass on the hearth. "You have to know something about him that will help," she persisted. "Something. If you don't, I have no place to start. I have nothing to take back to Tess. We'll never know why our parents separated us, why they lied to us. My sister was shot a couple of weeks ago trying to help me clear our father's name. It's my fault she's lying in a hospital. Her mother—our mother—is missing, last seen with your father. I just need to know if there's anything in his past that would put my mother in jeopardy. For instance, when did he change his name to Swope? Why?"

"I don't know, Katie. He was using his real name when he was here," Nick said. "He said he was on an extended vacation. He seemed a little nervous. I told him to get lost, but Patricia fell for his story. He was reformed, he claimed. No more drinking. No more shenanigans. All he wanted was to get to know his long-lost son. Me. And Patricia and Lily, of course. Patricia's mother had died the year before and she was anxious for more family. She invited him to stay in one of the guest cottages. He moved right in and made himself at home."

"How did you handle it?"

"I ignored him most of the time. It was summer and we had a bunch of people here. I was in and out. Busy."

"Your wife taught art during the summers?"

"Patricia? No. Patricia didn't teach art. We bought the place because I'm a pilot. The people who come here during the summer come because of me. I fly them over wilderness areas and they shoot wildlife. Photo shoot, I mean. Patricia's art was personal, not commercial. She wouldn't sell any of her work."

"They're all over your walls, aren't they?"

He looked around him. "Yes."

"They're beautiful."

"She was good. Now the paintings belong to Lily. Anyway, that summer after Lily was born, Patricia discovered gardening. She grew cabbages big as a barbeque, broccoli, carrots—this area of Alaska has long, cool summer days, up to twenty hours long, perfect for certain vegetables. Patricia was dedicated to gardening. She could dig in the dirt forever, Lily napping nearby on a blanket. She hummed when she gardened. Off-key."

He sighed deeply before adding, "I was away much of the time my father was here. He started helping Patricia with Lily— Helen only worked a few hours a day helping out with the daily cabin cleanings and things like that back then. Patricia got to depending on my father. I even started to think he might have changed."

He chanced a look at Katie. She regarded him closely, her blue eyes sparkling with reflections of the lanterns around her. She said, "What happened, Nick?"

He shrugged. His throat closed for a second and he stared into the fire. Could he see this through?

He said, "Patricia was walking down Frostbite's main street with my father one afternoon. A car went out of control right in front of the grocery store. Patricia was seriously injured. Dad walked away without a scratch. The driver of the car recovered and took off like a shot. Thank goodness Lily was here with Helen and not in her mother's arms. Patricia died twelve hours later without ever regaining consciousness."

"So you blame your father for living through the accident?" she murmured.

He cut her a quick look. "Of course not. I blame my father for leaving town while my wife was still lying on the pavement. I blame him for leaving her alone to die."

She nodded, tears glistening in her eyes and he used the act of tending the fire to regain his composure.

"So, next thing I know I get a wedding invitation from your mother," he said, turning back to face her. "Helen tried to hide it from me, but I found it anyway. A few weeks after that, your sister sent me a picture of the happy couple."

She sat forward eagerly. "Do you still have it? I haven't seen her—"

"I'm sorry," he said. "I tore it in half the minute I realized what it was."

"And now he's changed his name and gotten another woman to believe in him," Katie said, coming to stand beside Nick as he replaced the poker.

The firelight shimmering in her red hair made it glow like rubies. Her skin was white and soft looking, her eyes big and blue. A tingling sensation ran through Nick's hands. It had been over two years since he'd touched a woman's face, since he'd come close to even thinking about touching a woman's face. The urge to do so now was almost unbearable.

But why this woman?

He said, "Why do you limp?"

"I was in a hit-and-run accident. It had to do with my trying to figure out what happened to my father."

"And did you figure it out?"

She rolled her head a little as though her

neck hurt. "No, my sister figured it out for me. She came from out of the blue and probably saved my life."

"Does your neck hurt?"

"Yes. Another leftover from the accident."

He gently turned her around until her back was to him and began rubbing her shoulders with strong hands.

"That feels wonderful," she whispered.

He realized at once he'd attempted to satisfy his desire to touch her by approaching her in this no-nonsense, impersonal manner. Lots of layers of clothes under his fingers, no eye contact. He said, "What do you mean when you say your sister came from out of the blue?" *But, dear God, her hair was soft as it brushed against the back of his hands. And the supple warmth of her neck.*

"I'm warning you, it's a soap opera," she said softly, leaning into his hands.

"Try me."

"Okay, but like I said, it's a soap opera. My parents divorced when Tess and I were barely six months old. Mom took Tess. Dad took me. Neither told us we even had an identical twin sister only a day or two days' drive away. We didn't even know we had another parent. Dad told me my mother died giving birth and Mom told Tess she'd never even known Tess's father's last name. Then my father, a cop, died in a fire he was blamed for starting. I had to vindicate him. I found a letter from my dad telling me about my sister's existence. When I was hurt, she was contacted. She found me in a coma and took up my investigation. Now she's been shot and she's in the hospital and we've only really known each other for a few days."

"She helped you with your father and now you're determined to help her with her mother."

"Our father, our mother. My sister, myself. Yes."

He stopped massaging her neck and turned her back around to face him. Again, the urges, but this time it went beyond touching. This time he wanted to kiss her.

This is why he'd been annoyed with her from the moment he set eyes on her at the airport. He was afraid of her and not just because she threatened to bring the past crashing down on his home, but also because she'd so effortlessly cracked open doors long ago slammed shut.

"I have a feeling," she said softly, and it

was all he could do to take his gaze from her lips.

He said, "Yes?"

"I have a feeling that your father's past is catching up with him and that my mother is in the way."

He caught his hands sliding down her arms and let go of her. She didn't seem to notice. He said, "You may be right."

"I'm sorry I came here. I should have kept nagging the Washington police. I'll go home as soon as I figure out how to get back to Anchorage."

"I'll fly you back," he said, still under her spell, wishing things were different, wishing he could ask her to stay, to forget about her mother and his father, just stay for a while and...

And what?

He said, "I'm sorry I can't help you, Katie Fields."

For a moment they stared into each other's eyes. Nick had no idea what Katie was thinking. He just knew his own thoughts were jumping from pillar to post. Hopefully a good night's sleep would get him back to normal. It sounded as though the storm was abating a bit; his salvation would lie in the weather clearing so he could fly Katie away from Frostbite.

"I—" she started to say, but a sound outside caught both their attention and they turned as one to face the door.

"Was that—"

"Gunfire," he finished for her, quickly drawing her away from the fireplace into the deeper recesses of the house. "Yes."

"Nearby?"

"Yes." He tore open a closet and shone a flashlight inside. The gun safe was back there and he twirled the combination.

"You any good with a firearm?" he asked over his shoulder.

In a shaking voice, she said, "I've shot off a few rounds with my dad."

He emerged with a Winchester 30-30 and a 20-gauge automatic shotgun. He inserted ammunition into each weapon before pushing the shotgun toward Katie.

She took the shotgun with trembling hands. She looked scared to death but reassuringly resolute. "What's the plan?" she asked.

"The plan? I go outside and see what's going on. You stay here and lock the door behind me. That's the plan."

"I know how to shoot—"

"Katie? Someone has to stay inside and protect Lily." He said this while retrieving his jacket and shrugging it on, zipping the front, pulling on his knit cap.

"You're not going out there by yourself!"

She wanted to go with him? Startled by this realization, he half smiled. He said, "Someone has to go out in that storm and find out who's shooting at who. I believe I may be the more qualified. Please, Katie, keep Lily safe."

Before he could consider the wisdom of his action, he brushed her forehead with his lips. "Lock the door behind me," he whispered, turning off the lantern and sliding the dead bolt back. "Don't let anyone but me back inside the house."

And then he was gone.

Chapter Five

As Nick blended into the shadows, Katie heard a new volley of shots, muffled by the snow. She stepped over the threshold into the night. She had a shotgun, she could probably hit something—or someone—and it seemed wrong for Nick to be out there alone with heaven knows what. Or whom.

But his parting words, his overriding need to protect Lily, stopped her mid-step. Another shot, a voice, someone crashing through the brush…

She stepped back inside, stumbling as haste made her clumsy. Pain shot up her leg as she pushed the dead bolt home.

What in the world had she gotten herself into by coming to this house? There had been a man at the window—it was too much of a coincidence to believe that a stranger had peered inside the house just an hour before shots were fired outside. What did she know of Nick's personal life? Maybe there was a jealous husband out there or someone connected to Helen.

She tried to find comfort in the totally effortless way Nick handled weapons, but comfort was elusive when it came to Nick.

How about the way he looked at you, the way he kissed your forehead, the way your heart battered against your ribs when his lips touched your skin, when his hands clenched your arms, brushed your neck?

No comfort. This place was a nuthouse. And she was turning out to be the biggest nut of all.

Katie limped down the hall to check on Lily and found the child asleep, her pink lips pursed in some dream, her breathing slow and regular. Katie sat down on the foot of Lily's bed, the shotgun across her knees, straining to hear gunshots over the raucous sounds of the storm.

To her horror, her movement awoke the child, who sat up whimpering, eyes closed.

Katie immediately laid the gun aside and scooted closer to Lily, who held out her arms. Katie wrapped Lily in a warm embrace and smoothed her hair, whispering nonsensical murmurs to comfort her, rocking her in her arms. Within minutes, Lily's heavy head signified she'd fallen back asleep without actually waking up, and Katie gently laid her head back on her pillow, covering her shoulders, not even trying to resist the urge to kiss her forehead and smooth her hair away from her face.

What a darling, sweet child. Nothing must happen to her.

Or to her father.

Standing, Katie retrieved the shotgun and moved out of the bedroom, closing the door. She went back through the house, turning off many of the flickering lanterns, bathing the house in darkness except for the fireplace, which filled the living room with leaping shadows. She stood by the front door and listened. When had she heard the last shot? How long should she wait before going outside and looking for Nick? What if he'd been wounded or…or worse.

Her hand rested on the doorknob as she pressed her head against the wood. What should she do? Indecision was a new sensation for her. Usually, she reacted first and celebrated—or regretted—later. But never before had she been even marginally responsible for someone else. Someone innocent. Someone like Lily. And so far on this endless day, she'd done the impulsive—and wrong—thing almost one-hundred percent of the time.

Except she hadn't thrown herself into Nick's arms when he'd looked at her that way; she hadn't even let him know she wanted to. She'd been mature and reasonable when he massaged her shoulder, when he turned her to face him, when he said her name and it sounded like the beginning of a song. She hadn't allowed a single emotion to bubble to the surface.

And maybe that was the biggest mistake of the night.

Her headache was back with a vengeance.

NICK STAYED CLOSE to buildings and snow-covered vegetation as he crept toward the sound of gunfire. There were two weapons at play; one sounded like a single-fire revolver, the other an automatic of some kind.

So, who in the world would be conducting a gunfight outside his house in the middle of the night during a snowstorm? And what were the chances this nocturnal shoot-out wasn't connected directly or indirectly to Katie Fields's arrival in Frostbite?

Was she in danger? Had she put Lily in danger?

He shoved thoughts of Katie and Lily aside. It was imperative he put a stop to whatever was going on out here before it erupted into his house. Keeping his head down, he waited until more shots rang out before moving across a patch of exposed snow, zigzagging as he'd been taught so many years before, catching his breath as he found a tree to hide behind. He heard one man yell, another swear. The labored sound of heavy breathing seemed very close by and he chanced another look.

Two men stood a hundred feet to his right, facing each other. They fired at the same time. One bullet hit its mark and the man closest to Nick fell to the snow. The other gunman turned and, slogging through the snow, ran back into the shadows.

Nick's fingers were so cold they were stiff as they clutched the rifle. He should have put on gloves. He was stunned that he'd forgotten such a basic necessity. These thoughts zipped through his mind as he stared at the fallen man.

Taking a roundabout approach, he made his way to the dark shape lying in the snow. As he came within a few feet, he heard more rapid fire. He was under attack! As bullets whizzed behind him, he tumbled forward in the snow, the rifle held out at the side, scrambling to his knees to take cover behind the wounded man, shooting into the brush near the dock from where the shots came.

The injured man groaned. Nick couldn't risk even the smallest of flashlights to check for wounds. He used his frozen hands and felt something warm and sticky on the man's chest.

Time was critical. Did he have an injured good guy, an injured bad guy or what?

He shook the victim's shoulder and got more groans. Obviously, the wound was too extensive to make this man much of a threat. Nick would get him into the house; to leave him out here would be to leave him to die from exposure.

He rose to a stooped position. In the moment of stillness that followed, he heard the crunch of someone approaching through snow. Breathing suspended, he searched the landscape.

Another shot and a bullet sliced through his jacket sleeve. Nick returned fire and a dark shape detached itself and fell forward from a bank of trees.

Nick stood slowly, shakily. It had been well over ten years since he'd fired a gun at another human being. He used the small flashlight he always carried in his pocket to examine the fallen man in front of him. Blood seeped through his jacket. His face was covered with fallen snow.

Nick then moved to the other man, rifle ready. This guy was lying on his face. A 9mm Glock had fallen beside his hand and Nick picked it up carefully, thumbing on the safety, dropping it into the deep pocket of his down jacket.

He could feel no pulse, but his hands were so cold it was hard to know for sure. Since his sympathies at this point favored the first wounded man, who at least hadn't shot at him, Nick retraced his steps, shining his flashlight. The injured man flung up an arm in a defensive gesture—a good sign. Nick stooped to help him stand, supporting most of his weight. Helping the victim manage the deepening snow quickly became an arduous chore made more difficult as the poor guy lost consciousness.

When Nick finally gained the front porch, he pounded on the door. There wasn't time for finesse. He yelled, "Katie? Let me in."

She had apparently been hovering against the door, for the moment his hand hit the solid wood, it flew inward. She seemed to size up the situation in a heartbeat. Throwing her shoulder under the man's other arm, she helped Nick get him inside and onto a leather sofa. For a small woman, she was strong, though Nick did notice her limp was back.

Sweeping a lap blanket off one of the chairs, he gave it to Katie with the instructions, "Apply pressure to his chest. There's another injured man outside. I've got to get to him before he freezes."

His gaze followed hers as it dropped to his arm. A rent in the sleeve leaked white down.

"Nick, what's going on?"

"Gunfight at the OK corral," he said. Seeing the bewilderment in her eyes, he added, "Two men are trying to kill each other. And me. I'll be right back." He turned when he reached the door to find Katie leaning over the man on the couch, pressing the blanket against his chest. Her complexion had turned a pea-soup green.

Nick retraced his steps, using the flashlight to illuminate the night. The snow seemed to be slowing down. He found the scuffed-up snow he'd created as he helped the fallen man stand upright and veered off toward the trees, looking for the man he'd brought down with his rifle.

He found a depression in the snow, spatters of cherry-red blood, and the barest trace of footsteps leading away. The man hadn't been dead after all.

Nick had the gunman's Glock in his pocket, but there was nothing to say there wasn't another gun trained on him at that very moment. He immediately flicked off the light and hugged the landscape again, making his way back to the house in a hurry. Just before he opened the door, he thought he heard the sound of a motor starting off toward the south. He paused, listening. Yes, a motor.

"Where's the other one?" Katie asked as he locked the front door behind him.

"Gone. I wounded him, but he apparently wasn't as bad off as I thought," he said shrugging off his jacket.

"This one is a mess," Katie said.

Nick said, "Well, we'll do what we can for him." He moved closer. Katie had used a corner of the blanket to wipe the man's face clear of snow.

Nick said, "I heard a motor start. Probably a—"

He stopped talking as he took in the haggard face of the wounded man lying on his sofa.

Time seemed to stop.

It just stopped. A minute, two minutes… a week.

"Nick? What is it? Do you know this man?"

"Yes," Nick whispered, breathing again, blinking.

"Who is he? Nick?"

"My father. This man is my father."

"Your father!" She stood abruptly, her face drained of color, her hands covered with blood. Nick took over with the blanket.

"If this is your father, then where in the hell is my mother?"

Chapter Six

Caroline surveyed her "cell" on hands and knees, shaking with fear and cold, her thin pajamas little help in keeping warm.

One wall, a right angle, another wall, another turn, another wall. A small pipe, flush with one wall, allowing cold, fresh air to seep into the pit. Her hands bumped against something freestanding and solid and she stopped. Sitting with her back against the dirt wall, she patted the floor with eager fingers to recover what she'd bumped into.

Something heavy—a plastic jug. Two. Three. Then something soft like clothing—no, a blanket. A small box filled with objects. Fumbling in the box, she felt a cool, metal cylindrical shape. A flashlight, she realized with a stab of relief so acute it forced a sob from her throat. She flicked it on with a surge of hope.

The hope died as she shone the light over four dirt walls and a roof that looked as though it was composed of sheets of plywood. Her prison was little more than a four-foot-deep hole in the ground. She beat against the boarded top and was rewarded with dense thuds. Even though there were a few gaps in the boards, they didn't admit any light.

Her total findings consisted of three gallon bottles of water, an empty pail with a lid, presumably for waste, a roll of tissue, two rough wool blankets that looked like Army surplus, a box of crackers, two dozen plastic-wrapped cheese sticks and five green apples.

The volume of food alarmed her. There was so much! Did this mean she was going to be held here for several days?

She'd spent a lifetime trying to get away from her thoughts. The realization that they were to be her only company for who knows how long caused her heart to race—the sure beginning of a panic attack.

She held the flashlight against her chest, afraid to turn it off even though she'd found no extra batteries. What did it matter? Better to have light now, better to investigate every nook and cranny, better to examine the wooden "lid."

If she yelled through the cracks? Through the pipe?

Up on her haunches, she pressed her lips against the wood and screamed. She hit it with her fists. When that proved pointless, she screamed into the pipe. Nothing. Next she examined the walls with the flashlight. None of this flurry of activity revealed any new information, and once again she sank into a sitting position, tears running unheeded down her cheeks. She wrapped one blanket around her shoulders and another around her legs. She tried conjuring up Bill's face, Tess's face. She needed them. But she couldn't see more than their eyes, and their eyes were filled with disappointment.

She turned off the flashlight and was instantly plunged back into darkness.

Bill and Tess were a million miles away.

She was totally alone.

Who was doing this to her?

And *why*?

"DOES HE LOOK like the man you saw at the window?" Nick asked as stared down at his father.

"I don't know. It's kind of hard to tell."

"Well, I guess we better try to save him," Nick said, turning away.

While retaining pressure on the injured man's wound, Katie carefully cut away the thick layers of clothes covering his torso. Meanwhile, Nick relit the lanterns, heated water on a butane burner and gathered medical supplies. He seemed to have an abundance of the latter and explained that living in a town without a doctor meant taking care of small emergencies yourself.

Small emergencies.

Nick's father groaned and Katie stopped what she was doing in order to pay close attention to his mumbling. Nonsensical sounds that may or may not have been words. Eyes opening and closing without comprehension, more murmurs and groans. Somewhere inside this man's head was the knowledge of where Katie's mother could be found. It had to be in there. He had to live to share it. He had to live long enough to tell them where to start looking.

"Where is she, where's my mother?" Katie urged. "Bill, where is Caroline?"

"Caroline," he muttered, but that was all he got out before he faded away again.

Nick deposited a tray of supplies on the nearby table. He'd already positioned four lanterns to shed as much light as possible. "I don't think he's up to much conversation," he said.

"No kidding." Catching sight of the scalpel on the tray, she added, "Do you actually have medical training?"

"Not really. You?" He pulled a stool close.

"None. His breathing seems shallow."

"He's probably going into shock. I should have made a stretcher to get him inside, but the bullets whizzing past my head made me a tad anxious."

She stared at Nick for a moment. "I know you don't like your father, that he's disappointed you in the past," she said, "but you have to put that behind you. It's time to mend fences and—"

"Please, please," he interrupted. "Spare me the psychobabble."

"You have to save him," she insisted.

He didn't look particularly convinced.

"I mean it, Nick. Without him, we have absolutely no clue as to where to start looking for my mother."

"I'm not an idiot and I'm not into patricide," he scoffed.

"Just so you understand."

"I understand. I have to save my father in order to save your mother. I got it."

She looked away. All she knew was that if Bill opened his eyes and saw the expression on his son's face and the scalpel in his hand, he'd probably pass out again.

Together they peeled away the blood-soaked garments, exposing the bullet hole. "It's a little higher on the chest than I thought it was," Nick said briskly. "That's good—it probably bypassed anything major. If it hit the carotid artery, he'd have already bled out." He rolled his father gently onto his side. "There's no exit wound though. I'm not a surgeon, but I think the bullet better come out."

"Can you do that?"

"I'd better try." He brought a syringe from his medical kit and injected his father with morphine.

The next thirty minutes were a nightmare for Katie, though Nick seemed to enter into a focused zone that precluded anything but the task at hand. He sliced through his father's skin and muscle with apparent calm, attempting to find the bullet that had torn through the older man's flesh. When he finally dropped the squat piece of metal onto the tray, Katie swallowed hard and did her best not to faint.

When he was finished, Katie taped on layers of bandages while Nick carried away the bloody towels.

"This will have to do until we can move him to a hospital," Nick said, standing back and surveying their handiwork.

"When will that be?"

"As soon as the storm lets up and the roads are usable."

"It's too bad my sister wasn't able to come up here instead of me," Katie said as she peeled off the sterilized gloves both she and Nick had worn.

"Why?"

"She's a veterinarian. She'd have been a lot more help to your father than a bartender."

"Is that what you do?"

"I've done that and a few other odd jobs."

"No focus?"

She sighed. "No money."

"So what would you like to do?"

"In my fantasy world? Run a place of my own. A little bar with a restaurant. Good food, nice music, friendly people. I took a few business courses at night at junior college, so maybe someday… Right now, I wish I'd taken premed."

"No kidding. Well, I think that's all we can do for now." After they'd cleaned up and wrapped Nick's father in more blankets, Nick added logs to the fire. It was two in the morning and Katie was dead on her feet, but a new thought struck her as she looked out the window.

"What if she's out there?" she whispered.

Nick had just come back into the room after checking on Lily. "At least it stopped snowing," he said.

"Nick, what if she's out there? My mother, I mean. Maybe she was hit by one of the bullets before you even went outside."

"I hadn't thought of that." He turned resolutely and started putting his snow gear back on.

"I'll come with you," Katie said.

"Lily—"

"I'll check back in on her."

He gestured at his father. "What if he says something about what happened, about where your mother is?"

They both looked at the man. "He's not going to say anything for a while," Katie said resolutely.

He regarded her with a strange expression on his face. "Is there anything at all that you're afraid of?"

"Yes," she said. "Snakes."

"What kind?"

"What do you mean, what kind? All kinds."

"They're a necessary part of the ecosystem. Without them—"

"Nick? Save it. You asked, I'm telling. Snakes."

He laughed. "Well, you're in luck. It's way too cold to find many snakes slithering about."

Katie bundled up in her own coat, but borrowed gloves and boots from Helen's stash in the washroom. They checked on Lily, who was sleeping soundly, then locked her inside the house with plans to take turns every few minutes to check on her and on Nick's father. Nick helped Katie into a pair of snowshoes then put on some himself.

Armed with the shotgun and a huge, powerful flashlight, Katie covered the front, including the cabins, all of which were empty and cold. Her leg throbbed with the effort of walking, difficult even with the snowshoes. She searched nearby fences and trudged through the small meadow, careful to avoid mounds, which she'd discovered were usually snow-covered bushes that collapsed when she got too close, trapping her snowshoes until she dug them out. It was a slow, tedious, painful procedure.

Nick, meanwhile, took care of the area out by the lake. Eventually, they both investigated the boathouse. The structure was big and dark and filled with watercraft and summer paraphernalia, making it almost impossible to find every hiding spot. It didn't help that their only source of illumination came from flashlights.

Nick discovered one thing—his phone line had been sliced in two. He swore when he saw it.

"I wonder when that got cut."

"That's the million-dollar question," he said. "Let's get back inside the house."

In the end, Katie had to agree. If her mother was outside, she was well hidden.

Or dead.

NICK LED THE WAY back into the house where they once again checked on Lily and his old man, stoked the fire and retreated to a pair of armchairs in the far corner.

He figured if he looked half as weary as Katie did, they made a pair to draw to.

"Well, he's done it again," Nick said, glancing across the room at his father who, wrapped in blankets and lying still as stone, resembled a mummy more than a living man.

"He's brought trouble into your life," Katie said.

Nick nodded, running a hand through his sandy hair. "There's one person we've kind of forgotten about," he said.

"I assure you, I haven't forgotten about my mother for an instant—"

"Not your mother. The man I shot earlier tonight. What's to keep him from coming back with reinforcements? Without being able to talk to my father about what's going on, we don't know who he was or what he wanted."

"Is it possible he was connected to the police?"

"No."

"How can you be so sure?"

"He shot at me first, Katie. Lawmen don't shoot at innocent people without issuing a warning of some kind."

She jumped to her feet and walked back

over to his father, staring down at him. It looked to Nick as though she was willing him to wake up.

Good for her. If the power of her single-minded desire had any magic in the world, perhaps it would manifest itself right then and there with his father's return to consciousness.

His father might open his eyes and tell Katie where her mother was. Then Nick could kindly shuffle them both out of Alaska to find the dear lady, and his life would go back to normal.

He bent his elbow on the chair arm and rested his forehead in his hand. After two years of peace and tranquility, he was sorely out of practice for nonstop drama. Within the past twelve hours he'd been subjected to Katie Fields's iron will, Helen's irrational behavior and subsequent desertion, a gunfight resulting in two people down, a mad gunman on the loose plotting heaven knows what, discovering his father had returned and doing his best to dig a bullet out of the old man's shoulder. What next? Fire? Pestilence?

"How did the two men get to your house?" Katie said.

She'd moved to stand in front of his legs and was looking down at him, hair falling forward, expression intense. Patricia had stood just like that off and on through their marriage, mainly when she'd been annoyed with him. Back then, he'd yank on her hands until she tumbled into his lap and gave up being mad because it was so much nicer being happy.

Out of the question with this woman. He said, "Snowmobiles probably."

"Did you hear a motor start up after you carried your father back to the house?"

"As a matter of fact, I did. I heard some kind of four-stroke engine and I'm assuming that's what it was. Why else do you think I allowed you to go outside with me to search for your mother?"

"You allowed me?"

"Anyway," he said, "what's your point?"

"Wouldn't they have to wear snowshoes or something, to get from their machines to your house? It's hard work slogging through the snow. So where are their snowshoes? And there would have to be two vehicles, right? I mean, they certainly didn't come together. Why didn't we find the one your father used?"

"Maybe my father got here before the storm," he said, remembering the sound of the swinging gate out by the boathouse. He'd noticed it right after tucking Lily into bed and had assumed Helen had been walking on the pier. Could his father have arrived in Frostbite hours earlier; could he have hidden out in the boathouse; could his have been the face Katie saw in the window?

"We have to leave here as soon as it's light," he added. "We won't wait for the roads to be cleared. We'll take the snowmobile to the airport."

"What about your father—"

"I have a sled I can tow with the bigger machine."

"But can your plane take off in the snow?"

"If the sky is clear, I can take off. Don't worry about it. We can't sit here and wait for another attack. It's too dangerous."

"I don't know if your father can survive—"

"My father needs a real doctor. It may be his best chance for survival and, as you remind me every other moment, your mother's chances rely on his chances."

She sat back in the chair. "I don't know—"

Now he popped to his feet. "*You* don't need to know," he said firmly. "*I* know. This is my house, my child. I will not gamble on her well-being. Don't go getting some crazy idea in your head that my father showing up changes anything. My one and only priority is Lily. I'm not going to rush to anyone's rescue if it means Lily is put in danger."

Katie was back on her feet. "You are the most egotistical man I've ever met. I don't need you."

"Good."

"I assumed you were a man of honor—"

"Don't talk to me about honor," he said, his voice low.

She took a deep breath. "I understand your need to protect your daughter, Nick, I do," she said. "But don't you understand my need to save my mother? She's an innocent victim in this, too, you know."

He stared at her for a moment, his irritation fading quickly as she once again stood close enough to touch. "Yes, I know," he said, his hands moving without his permission, landing on her shoulders. "The battlefield is always littered with innocent victims," he said softly as he momentarily lost himself in her blue eyes.

She smiled slowly. "Nick?" she said. "Just kiss me, okay?"

Had some trick made it sound as though she'd invited him to—

"Just do it."

"I...I don't want to kiss you," he mumbled, suddenly intensely embarrassed. It was bad enough to have these feelings simmering on the back burner of his mind; having her acknowledge them was terrible. "We're in the middle of an argument," he snapped.

"I know we are. But maybe if we just kiss, then we can get past wanting to and then we won't argue."

"That's the stupidest thing I've ever heard."

"Oh, for heaven's sake," she said, and standing on her tiptoes, put her arms around his neck and forced his head down toward hers.

"Give it your best shot," she whispered with a wicked smile.

"This is a bad idea," he muttered, though he couldn't hear his own words over the drumming of his heart.

Her lips moved. He had no idea what she said, just that her grip didn't relax.

The past few hours of irritation, surging adrenaline and time out of place all collided in that moment. And now this bewitching redhead with the nerves of steel and the brashness of a sailor was making him feel things he'd sworn he'd never feel again.

And so he gave in to temptation and kissed her just as he'd wanted to do for hours. Her lips were as sweet as he'd suspected they would be, the longing to kiss her again as strong as he'd feared.

"Now you've started something," he said against her cheek, trailing kisses up to her eyes and across her forehead, his fingers tenderly caressing her neck and jaw. It was as though he'd never touched a woman before, his fingertips registered the silken feel of her skin as a new experience.

She released her hold on him and moved a step away. "My intention was to *stop* something," she said, her eyes wide. He was oddly pleased to find that she no longer looked so damn smug.

"It didn't work," he said. "More like dousing fire with kerosene."

"We need to go to bed," she said. When he smiled, she added, "We need actual sleep, not what you're thinking. I don't even know you, and besides, we're kind of related."

"Like hell we are."

She glanced at her watch. "How are you

going to fly a plane if you're so tired you can't see straight?"

Thanks to her proximity, he wasn't tired at all, which, when he thought about it, alarmed him. He moved a few steps away, throwing discreet glances at every dark corner of the room in an effort to find his reflection anywhere else but in her eyes. He'd been flirting with her, he admitted to himself, acting playful. Maybe he was tired. Maybe that's what was wrong with him.

"Go to bed," he said without meeting her eyes. "I'll stay out here to make sure the bad guys don't kill us in our sleep."

In the end, she did as he suggested and took a lantern down the hall. He settled in on one of the red chairs, a book open on his lap, his eyes flitting over strings of words that made no sense, because his mind was racing with the events of the past few hours.

Then again, very little made sense right then.

However, it wasn't long before the day's activities began to catch up with him and he found himself yawning. His father's even breathing, thanks probably to the morphine, didn't help. Nick got up at last and heated water for instant coffee and then he went down the hall to check on Lily.

But Lily wasn't alone in her bed. Katie had fallen asleep next to his daughter, fully clothed, red hair spilled across his daughter's extra pillow, the spare down blanket covering her body.

For one blinding instant he was furious with Katie for—intruding. That was it. She'd taken far too many liberties. But the moment of ire was as brief as it was intense, and his next emotion caught him in a stranglehold.

They looked so right lying there together. A woman with a big heart and strong convictions and a child with her mother's face and zest for life, a child without a mother whose hand lay curled in Katie's relaxed palm.

Katie was worming her way into his house, his heart, his child's life. The feel of her lips still burned on his, the ache for her that he'd glossed over with humor still lingered like a battle wound that wouldn't heal.

He had to put a stop to this. He couldn't be the hero Katie wanted, the hero she needed. He couldn't take a chance of leaving Lily alone in the world, he couldn't risk…

Risk. That's what it amounted to.

Terrible risk.

He left the room with a heavy heart. When Katie woke up he'd have to be firm; he'd have to make her understand. He'd get her and his dad to safety. That's all.

Beyond that, he could do no more.

Chapter Seven

"Who's that?"

Nick opened his eyes quickly, sitting up in his chair, blinking. The room was still dark, though the faint light coming in the front window suggested the nine-o'clock sunrise was well on its way.

Two green eyes stared right into his. Lily whispered, "Daddy? Who's that man?"

Nick gathered his daughter in his arms as he stood. "That's just a man," he said.

"Where'd he come from?" she insisted, squirming in his arms to look over his shoulder.

Nick turned her to face his father, holding her close as though she was teetering on the edge of a high diving board. "From the snow," he said.

Her little mouth formed a perfect O as she whispered, "He's a real live snowman?"

"Who's a snowman?" This from Katie, who had come into the living room dressed as she'd gone to sleep—in jeans and sweater—her red hair mussed and utterly beguiling. He met her gaze.

"The man on the couch," Nick said, pleading with his eyes for Katie not to say the word *Grandpa*.

She apparently understood. "Is the…snowman…is he any better?"

"I don't know, I haven't had a chance to check," he said. Katie walked up to Lily and, opening her arms, said, "Come on, little one. Let's make breakfast. Something warm, okay?"

"Hot chocolate?" Lily said, launching herself into Katie's arms.

They left the room together, their voices intermingled, their laughter private.

Nick shook his head. Not the way he'd intended on starting the morning. His goal for the day was to get rid of his two houseguests, not to have Katie insert herself any more prominently into anyone's heart.

He knelt down beside his father, whose breathing seemed shallow and whose forehead felt warm to the touch. He'd developed a fever since the last time Nick had checked on him.

In a sudden motion that jarred Nick with its intensity, the older man grabbed Nick's wrist. His eyes flicked open. Green eyes, like Nick's, like Lily's. "Where—" he said, his lips dry, his speech slurred.

Nick withdrew his hand from his father's grasp and retrieved a glass of water. He held the glass to his father's lips and watched as the older man swallowed. His eyes drifted shut again as he mumbled, "Where am I?"

"You're at…my house," Nick said uneasily. How could he call himself this man's son? He couldn't. He wouldn't.

"Caroline," his father whispered. "Where is she?"

"I don't know," Nick said. "Don't you?"

A meager tear appeared at the corner of his father's eye, hovered on his cheekbone.

"And Carson?"

"Who's Carson?"

"Frank Carson. Was it…him? Did he… did he shoot me?"

"Probably. I don't know who Carson is. Why did he or someone else try to kill you?"

His old man grabbed his arm again. "I have to find Carson. I have to go…"

"You can't leave in your condition. Just talk to me. Did this Carson take Caroline?"

Bill shook his head and the tear rolled down the deep crease in his cheek.

"Did Carson—did he kidnap Caroline?" Nick insisted. "If so, where did he take her? Why did he take her?"

"I don't know," his father cried, tears rolling feely now.

Nick sat back on his heels. Why did he get the feeling his old man was lying?

"Where were you when she was abducted?"

Nick was suddenly aware that Katie had entered the room and was, in fact, standing nearby, eyes huge, body tense. He said to his father, "You have to give us a place to start looking for her. Someplace the police—"

The word *police* galvanized his father as nothing else had. His eyes took on a manic, feverish glow, and his hand on Nick's arm trembled. He seemed to age fifteen years in the blink of an eye. "No police. They'll kill her. Promise. No police."

Frustration, disbelief, fear, anger—a veritable witches' brew of emotions roiled in Nick's gut. This problem wasn't going to go away. If Katie's mother was in jeopardy and it was his father's fault, then where did Nick's responsibility begin and end? It had all seemed so clear-cut in the dead of the night. But now…

He couldn't turn his back on Katie or her mother, not if his father's behavior had caused their predicament, and not if his father knew more than he was saying. Nor could he jeopardize Lily's welfare.

He looked back in time to see his father's eyes close again, and this time there was a permanency to the action that convinced Nick there would be no further information for a while. He contemplated dispensing aspirin for the fever, deciding against it because of its blood-thinning properties. The wound no doubt needed rebandaging, but he wasn't sure. The little bits and pieces of medical training he'd received over the years had come and gone.

Lily toddled up to him, a vision in pink, and handed him a sloppy half-full cup of tepid hot chocolate. "For Mr. Snowman," she whispered.

He looked at his precious daughter as she unknowingly stared at her grandfather. He yearned to whisk her away, to turn back the clock a few days, a few years, to wrap her in cotton and put her somewhere safe.

Like where? Where was life safe?

And where was Katie?

He scanned the room and found her backed against the wall, her eyes glistening. For the first time in the short while he'd known her, she looked terrified. Their eyes met and, almost as though following an invisible line strung between them, she crossed the room, coming to a halt right before him.

He patted the chair seat and she sat down on the edge of the cushion.

He took her hands in his. "Katie?"

Impatient, Lily said, "Daddy? Mr. Snowman wants his hot chocolate. Wake him up!"

"Mr. Snowman is too sick for hot chocolate," Katie said softly. "Maybe your daddy would like it."

Lily produced a fetching grin. "Daddy can have it," she said, setting it down beside Nick before running back to the kitchen.

Nick glanced up at Katie. "I take it you heard—"

"I'm not sure what we should do," she said.

"For the time being at least, we don't call the police. But we have to get the snowman to a doctor."

"Could you fly your plane to another town

and get a doctor to come back here with you? Your dad looks too sick to make a trip—"

Nick shook his head. "I'm not leaving the three of you in this house by yourselves. The old man is burning up. He's either got an infection or I did something wrong when I dug out that bullet. I don't know if he'll make it until I get back here, and if another storm closes in and he dies or the man who shot him comes back—" He stopped talking. Katie looked a little green again.

"We'll leave together," he told her. "It's the only way. Get some food into Lily and yourself."

"How about you?"

"I'll eat later. Pack some of Lily's clothes, will you? I'll go make sure the snowmobiles are gassed up. Damn, we can't call the airport to see if the runway is clear. We'll have to take our chances."

"Snowmobiles? Nick, I've never driven a snowmobile in my life. I've never even ridden on one."

"There's a first time for everything," Nick said. He looked at her for another moment before throwing caution to the wind, leaning forward and briefly kissing her lips.

He wasn't used to treating caution in

such a cavalier way, wasn't used to acting on his feelings, and it made him squirm inside. "You're having an amazing effect on me," he said.

"I am?"

"I've never felt so confused in my life."

Looking directly into his eyes, she said, "Is that good or bad?"

"I don't honestly know. I thought I did. But now I don't."

"Good."

"Don't worry, I'll snap out of it. Someone has to keep a cool head, right? Might as well be me."

"Might as well," she agreed. "If it's not you, it's me and if it's me, my mom is doomed."

"Trust me, we'll find her," he said.

"But you—"

"Trust me," he said. He ran his fingers over her cheek and added, "We need to be ready to go as soon as possible."

"What about the man who shot your father? What if he's still out there?"

"We didn't get shot at when we looked for your mother, did we?"

"No, but that was hours ago. He's had time to go get his buddies and patch up the bullet hole you put in him. He might be cranky."

"We don't have a choice," Nick said.

THERE WAS A LOT to do. For Katie the time raced by as she packed clothes for Lily and food for everyone. How she longed for a phone so she could call Tess.

A more immediate concern, however, was the fact that Nick couldn't call the airport to check weather conditions. She tried to adopt his cool acceptance of the situation, marveling at the competent way he went about doing his tasks with a minimum of fuss. On the other hand, he'd left the care of his daughter—who turned out to have a very strong will when it came to what she would and would not wear—to Katie.

Sure, it was easy to be calm, cool and collected with an inanimate object like a gas can. But with a three-year-old who couldn't find her bunny?

Nick's father, pale, incoherent and still feverish, cried out as they rolled him onto a makeshift stretcher made out of canvas and carried him into the garage, where Nick had hooked a sled to the back of the biggest snowmobile. Nick gave him another shot of morphine and he quieted down, but the cost of that pain-free place for his father was several more hours of silence.

Inside Katie's head, questions circled like vultures over a rotting carcass: Who had kidnapped her mother? Where had they taken her? What did they want?

And why had Nick's father come to Nick for help? Surely he knew what kind of welcome awaited him here. And who was Carson and why was he shooting at Bill?

And why had Bill Thurman changed his name to Swope after Nick's wife died in an accident and before he wooed and married her mother?

Why, why, why?

After finally finding the bunny and zipping Lily into a yellow snowsuit with white fur trim around her face, Katie found Nick in the hall in the process of opening the gun safe. He put the handgun he'd recovered the night before in the safe along with the bullet he'd dug out of his father's shoulder. "In case this ever goes to trial," he told Katie, and then retrieved two different handguns, loaded them, made sure Katie understood about the safety, and helped her put on an over-the-shoulder holster.

"I feel I'm getting ready for a shoot-out,"

she said, as she slipped the gun into the holster.

"Precaution," he said, arming himself in a similar fashion.

"I thought you were sure—"

He shook his head. "Katie? I'm not sure about a single damn thing anymore."

He didn't preface that statement with *Thanks to you*, but it was there in his voice and in the look he gave her. She shut up.

Katie received a crash course in driving a snowmobile without actually moving one or even turning on its engine as they were inside the garage. She'd driven her father's motorcycle in the past, so it wasn't completely new. Still, she was very relieved when Nick tucked Lily into one corner of the sled. It would be bad enough to bash in her own head without taking Lily with her. She pulled on the full-face helmet and approached the smaller machine.

Nick said, "No, you're driving the big one."

She had to have heard him wrong. Must be the helmet. She took it off. Surely he wasn't asking her to be responsible for a wounded man and a tiny little girl? She said, "You're kidding."

"I'll go before you at first, but I may

circle. If we run into trouble, I'll need to maneuver. If I go down, you just keep your nose pointed southeast. There's a compass on the dash. If someone tries to shoot you, don't be shy, shoot him back. Okay?"

"But Nick—"

"This is the only way," he said.

"But if there are a lot of them—"

"I've been thinking about that," he told her, lowering his voice and moving them both away from Lily, who was also wearing a helmet. "My father only mentioned one man. Carson. If this Carson had reinforcements, they would have stormed the house. Why risk letting us get outside? No, it's just the one man, I'm sure of it. He may be too hurt to take another shot at any of us. Hell, for all we know, he may have ridden off last night and died a hundred yards down the road. We'll play it safe. Trust me."

"It's not you I don't trust, it's me," she said.

"I guarantee you that at about ten degrees Fahrenheit, you won't come across one single snake."

She tried to conjure up a grin.

With a sigh, she put the helmet back on, ignoring the way her hands trembled, concentrating on Nick's swagger and sure movements as he helped Lily lie down and cover herself and her bunny with the thick quilt he tucked around her. He opened the garage and mounted the smaller snowmobile.

His ability would have to fuel her lagging confidence.

And then they were off.

Chapter Eight

The noise the powerful vehicles made as they tore away from the house shattered the post-storm stillness of snow-burdened tree limbs, icicles hanging from power lines and porch roofs, a blanket of pristine white snow that somehow made the dark morning seem lighter.

Katie concentrated on following Nick's tracks past the guest huts and down what had resembled a driveway the afternoon before. The area blended now with the rest of the field. The fruitlessness of the search they had conducted during the night to make sure Katie's mom hadn't been abandoned to the elements revealed itself. There were so many drifts, so many trees and hollows, so much land they hadn't covered and never could. Nick must have understood this, and yet he had tramped around out here just like she had.

The foreboding morning seemed to press down on their small caravan. Obviously, there would be more snow as the day advanced and Katie felt a sense of urgency born of concerns for the weather, terror for her mother's unknown plight and Nick's father's deteriorating condition. Add the possibility of a gunman, and presto, her nerves were jumping around like downed electrical wires.

They hadn't gone far when Nick waved her back with one hand as they approached the bridge that joined his property with the unplowed road. She slowed to a stop, assuming he was making sure the bridge was in good condition. It was too noisy to hear anything, but her heart jumped out of her chest as she saw Nick veer away at the last moment, grasp the rifle he'd strapped to his back and fire a few rounds toward the bridge, turning quickly as he did so, holding the rifle aloft and circling with his arm for her to turn around. She was vaguely aware of an explosion near the bridge, but soon it was behind her and she didn't dare chance a backward glance. Maneuvering the big machine in a wide circle, conscious of her priceless cargo, took all her attention.

Nick slowed to a stop a mile later after by-passing the boathouse. They'd taken a small road leading around the lake and into the wilderness. Tall, snow-covered trees defined the edges of the road though occasional downed branches required caution.

"What happened?" she asked, looking back the way they'd come. There were too many trees in the way to see anything at ground level, but a smudge of black smoke hovered in the distant sky.

"An ambush," Nick yelled as she came to a stop beside him. "I worried he might wait by the bridge. He popped up at the last moment."

"Did you hit him?"

"I don't think so. But I did get his snow-mobile, so he'll be stuck out here for a while."

"I wonder where he got a snowmobile. I mean, did he rent it in Frostbite? Is there a dealer? We could check."

"Does a man like that *rent* a machine?" Nick mused.

Katie, alarmed to find her teeth clattering together though she wasn't aware of being cold, didn't answer.

"Let's get going," he said quickly. "We

can check on things like that from the air. I want to get Lily away from here as fast as possible. Follow me carefully, Katie. This road isn't used anymore and I don't know what condition its bridge is in."

She nodded and once again they resumed their flight, only this time it was slower going. The narrow bridge they finally approached seemed to sag under the weight of the newly fallen snow. Nick insisted on first walking across it, coming back, carrying Lily across while Katie walked beside him, then driving both vehicles, one at a time, to the other side. It took a while but Katie humored him. What did she know about rickety old bridges?

Houses started showing up at last, closer together as they moved forward, most dark, others with huge oil drums fueling lights and warmth. Some activity could be seen—people shoveling paths to woodpiles, for instance—but again, the noise of her vehicle kept her suspended in a kind of bubble of solitude. Nick had fallen behind her, she guessed to better guard Lily, who had stayed quite still during the excitement and subsequent trip.

They finally entered a small neighborhood and Nick took the lead, coming to a stop in front of a red wood house with a steeply pitched roof. Smoke drifted upward from a chimney and a man wearing a blue parka and a furry hat with earflaps shoveled a path from his front door to the garage. None of the streets had been cleared yet, giving the modest neighborhood a unified, muted appearance. Even the various vehicles looked like harmless lumps of snow.

They came to a roaring stop and the man leaned on his shovel. "Hey, Nick. You come for Helen? She's inside with Joy."

"Thanks, Lloyd. I need to talk to Helen," Nick said, getting off his machine and unstrapping his helmet.

Before Lloyd could respond, Helen appeared at the door but didn't make a move to leave the porch. She'd thrown on a coat and hat and hugged herself as she stared at Nick's approach. Nick, looking over his shoulder, said, "Katie, keep a lookout for anyone coming from anywhere, okay?"

Katie nodded. She tried waving at Helen, who responded with a small nod of her head. Maybe her continuing aloofness had something to do with the fact that Katie currently wore some of Helen's warm snow clothing, even her extra pair of boots. She'd be willing to bet that Helen noticed this and didn't much care for it.

Oh, well. It didn't seem likely the two women were intended to be best buddies. Katie got off her machine and went to stand by Lily's shrouded shape. Peeling from the outside while Lily flailed from the inside, the little girl's face soon appeared.

"Bunny is hot," Lily said as Katie pulled back a last corner and found Lily's green eyes and the bunny's glass buttons staring up at her.

"Better make sure he stays that way, honey. Put your blanket back." She heard Lily softly singing to the bunny from under the covers and she smiled to herself as she scanned the road both ways and listened for a new motor sound.

Then she checked on Nick's father, who was still out like a light.

Meanwhile, Nick stood on the porch talking to Helen. He hadn't told Katie they would stop here first, but of course it made perfect sense. He couldn't risk Helen going out to the house and finding them gone, nor could he risk Helen being approached by the wounded gunman. Who knew what he would tell her and what she would unwittingly divulge?

But she hadn't expected to see Helen disappear inside the house and reappear a scant five minutes later with a duffel bag in tow; nor had she expected her to wave goodbye to Lloyd and climb aboard the smaller snowmobile.

Nick shuffled through the snow to where Katie stood near Lily. Lily heard her father's approach and popped out of the blankets. "Bunny is hot," she said.

Nick patted the bunny's head. "Tell him a story," he said. "It'll take his mind off the temperature."

"'Bout the birdie in the palm tree?"

"That one is sure to work, Sweet Pea. Put your head under the blanket again, we'll be leaving very soon."

"Promise?"

"Promise," he said.

The child once again covered her head with the blanket. Nick looked back at Katie and said, "Helen's aunt has a house in a little town south of here. The aunt is away visiting relatives but Helen has a ton of other family there. We're going to take Helen to her aunt's house, because it's not safe for her to stay here. It's no secret she works for me or who her sister is and it has yet to be explained why my father came to my house or who shot at him. Until we figure this out, she's better off away from here. A cousin will meet her at the airport."

Katie said, "You think of everything."

"I'm trying. You want to ride behind Helen or with me?"

"What do you think?" Katie said, strapping on her helmet again. She got on behind Nick, who started the engine, shattering the peace, kicking up snow as their little procession traveled away from Helen's sister's house. This time the trip was slightly more pleasant, at least for Katie. Nick made a dandy wind barrier. His back was warm against her front, and nestling against his solid body calmed her nerves.

They were met at the airport by a man wearing so many layers of clothes he walked like a penguin. His eyes were black, his face was ruddy. "Katie Fields, meet Sam Owens," Nick said, and Sam, hands stuffed in his pockets, smiled warmly at Katie, his round face chafed from exposure.

"Morning, ma'am," he said. "Saw you yesterday when you came in with Toby."

Turning his attention to Nick, he added, "If you're leaving this morning you'd better get out of here while you have a chance. Another storm is fixing to blow through."

"I know. I'll need your help towing the Beaver onto the runway."

"No problem." As he'd talked, he'd wandered back toward the trailer. "Who's this?" he asked, staring at Nick's father.

Lily popped out of her blankets and grinned. "He's Mr. Snowman!" she squealed.

Sam laughed.

"Actually, he's a stranger, got caught out in the storm," Nick said.

"He looks sick. You taking him to the doctor in Anchorage?"

"That's the plan. Say, did any other planes land in Frostbite yesterday?"

"Just one, right about noon, carrying two men and the pilot. I wasn't here when they landed. The pilot hitched a ride over to the motel and the two men told the wife they was visiting friends."

"Is it still here?"

"Right over there," he said, pointing at a red-and-white airplane whose wings were covered with snow.

"Is this guy one of the passengers?"

"I don't know for sure," Sam said.

Once inside Nick's hangar, Nick went to work removing the last three rows of seats. He explained he did this often during the summer in order to take people aloft to photograph wildlife. Katie tried to imagine winging over a glacier with the doors open and the seats removed, hanging on to a camera.

Once the seats were out, Katie and Nick lifted Nick's father into the plane, glad for the privacy the hangar provided to do this without Sam Owens watching. It was bad enough suffering Helen's disapproving stare. Katie had the distinct feeling Helen would have preferred they leave the older man out in the snow for the next storm to take care of. Permanently.

Lily sat in the pilot's seat with her bunny, pretending to drive while Helen squeezed herself into the co-pilot seat, as far away from Nick's father as humanly possible given the small cabin. She talked with Lily and laughed, but it was as though the rest of them didn't exist. It wasn't long before Sam had towed the plane into position and Nick had performed the preflight check. Katie kept an unofficial lookout for bad guys, Nick's rifle by her side.

Katie strapped Lily into a seat in the back beside her as Helen flatly refused to be anywhere near Nick's father. This meant that Lily babbled to Katie as they flew over the white landscape, her little hands dancing through the air as she spoke, her small body resting against Katie's arm, her giggles downright infectious.

Was it possible she'd only known this enchanting little girl less than a day? No wonder Nick was so determined to keep her safe. No wonder parents died to save their children.

Your mother didn't.

The thought came like a flash of lightning.

Your mother walked away from you. She and your father didn't value either you or Tess as individuals. You were just a matched set to be divided like halves of an apple.

"Well, Mom," Katie whispered to herself, glad for the cabin noise that covered her voice. "Your duplicate daughter is now trying to save your skin. You'd better hope I value you more than you did me."

Lily tugged on her sleeve. "Why are you crying?" she asked.

Katie took the child's small hand into her own. "I don't know, honey," she said, flipping away the tears.

"You just being silly?" Lily asked, her eyes so wide and innocent that Katie was moved to kissing her small fingers. "Yeah," Katie agreed. "I'm just being silly."

She dug a tissue out of her pocket and blew her nose. As she did this, she noticed Nick's father's gaze on Lily who was bouncing her bunny up and down on the seat. Katie slipped out of her seat belt and kneeled by the older man, who appeared more pale than ever.

"Are you warm enough?" she asked, tucking the blanket around his torso and hips, trying her best not to jar his shoulder. Despite the padding Nick had laid down on the floor, it was cold. She checked to make sure his knit cap covered his ears.

The effort of nodding caused a grimace to flash across his face.

Did he and Nick look alike? She studied his features for a moment and tried to decide. Add twenty or thirty years to Nick, frost his sandy hair and lessen its thickness, add a past of alcohol abuse and hard living. Take away Nick's firm jaw, keep the same green eyes. Don't forget the premature wrinkles that almost always signaled a lifetime spent smoking, and maybe. Maybe.

She opened a bottle of water and helped Bill Thurman—Swope—take a sip. "I have hot soup in a Thermos—"

"Not now," he whispered, adding, "The little girl. Is that…is she…Lily?"

"Yes," Katie said.

"Patricia's baby," he said, grief filling his eyes.

"Bill? What happened to Caroline?"

His gaze shifted to Katie and back to Lily. "You know Caroline?"

"I'm her daughter. Anything you can tell me—"

"Tess?" he interrupted, his expression baffled. "But your hair—"

"No, no, I'm not Tess, I'm Caroline's other daughter. I'm Katie."

Frowning, he mumbled, "I don't understand. There's…only…the one."

So, her mother hadn't told her new husband about abandoning Tess's twin so many years before. Katie said, "I'll explain later. Right now, I just need to know where I can find my mother."

"But I don't know," he said haltingly.

As Nick engaged the landing gear, the plane jounced and Bill groaned.

"Careful," Katie called out.

Nick answered with a terse, "Get back in your seat, Katie. We're getting ready to land."

"Just a minute," she yelled, and looking back at Bill, persisted. "Just tell me what you can remember."

"Men came," he said, his breath catching on every word. "Near Seattle. They grabbed Caroline out of our bed." He paused for several seconds before adding, "They knocked me to the floor, threatened me. I had to leave her, I had to go…"

"Katie! Please. Now," Nick demanded.

"You left her?" Katie hadn't intended on saying this. It escaped on its own, and with the uttered words came the fear of the night before when Nick had said his father had a history of leaving women at the first sign of trouble. She caught a sob and demanded, "What did they want from you?"

The interchange had seemed to leach the energy right out of the man. His eyes drifted shut and his lips trembled, but he didn't speak.

"Bill," she insisted, because she had to

know. She was afraid he would die and then they'd be lost. "What did they want?"

His eyes opened again, his eyes remained fixed—no, transfixed—on Lily.

Katie drew back. Why wouldn't he answer her question? Shame? Guilt?

Another jounce, another yell from Nick, and Bill's gaze suddenly flashed from Lily to Katie and stuck. Reaching up with a shaking hand, he grabbed her jacket, pulling her head toward his. "Where are we?" he gasped.

"In Nick's plane. Almost in Vixen Hill."

"No," he cried, his voice trembling, his eyes desperate. "No, go back, go back."

This time when Nick raised his voice, it sounded to Katie as though he was ready to climb into the back and forcibly haul her into her seat. "Now!" he yelled. She scooted back and buckled herself in.

Lily grabbed her hand as the wheels touched down.

Go back?

Why?

Chapter Nine

Helen's aunt lived in a town that made Frostbite look like a large metropolis. The storm
hadn't dropped much snow here and what
there was had been plowed aside so that the
roads were open. Helen's sister had agreed to
call their extended family and, consequently,
a cousin met her at the airport driving a big
truck. The cousin seemed content to wait in
the truck for Helen to join him.

It was apparent Nick and Helen had been
discussing something since landing that had
them both in a fit of temper. The cabin noise
had meant that almost one-hundred percent
of what was said in the front stayed in the
front, just as what Nick's father had muttered
in the back of the plane wouldn't have
reached any ears but Katie's.

Go back? Had she heard him right? Was
he delirious, was that it?

No, that wasn't it. His eyes had held a degree of clarity he hadn't shown before or after. The uneasy feeling they had missed something of importance out in Nick's boathouse came fluttering back.

She had to talk to Nick, but not in front of Helen.

Meanwhile, Helen said, "You have to let her come with me."

"Not in a million years," Nick said.

Katie listened without talking. She knew exactly who Helen meant.

"Nick? Think. Anywhere that man is, trouble follows. Lily can't be in the middle of it, she just can't. She'll be safe here at my aunt's house. She's been here before, My cousins have lots of little kids for her to play with. You get rid of…him…and then you come back and Lily will be safe. Please."

He shook his head again. He was standing on the tarmac, holding Lily tightly as though afraid she might disappear if he loosened his grip. She had both arms thrown around his neck and the picture the two of them created caused tears to gather behind Katie's nose.

Katie, too, had once been her father's little girl. It had been just him and her, he'd been the center of her universe. She'd thought he could do no wrong, and even later, even after a gambling addiction had distorted him and limited what he was able to offer her, he'd still been her daddy and she'd fought to vindicate him after his death.

With Tess's help, she'd succeeded. Sort of. But what right did she have to burst into Nick Pierce's life and ask him to risk everything for people he didn't know or care about?

She said, "Nick? Maybe Helen is right."

Turning his green eyes on her, he said, "Not you, too."

"Listen to her," Helen urged. "Now she's talking sense."

"Just get me and your father to a hospital in Anchorage. That's all you have to do. I'll take it from there."

"How?"

She shrugged. "I'll think of something. But we should get going. He's awfully pale. He rallied for a while, but he sank away when you landed."

Nick studied her face for a moment and she wished she knew him well enough to figure out what he was thinking.

"You'll be back in a couple of hours,"

Katie added. "Then you can go home and forget all about this."

His expression intensified. Finally, he turned back to Helen and said, "I guess she would be safer with you. And have a lot more fun."

"Yes," Helen said with obvious relief.

Looking now at Lily, he said, "How about it, Pumpkin? Would you like to stay with Helen for a while?"

To everyone's astonishment, especially Katie's, Lily pointed at Katie and said, "Will she stay with me?"

"No," Katie said, taking Lily's mittened hand in her own and squeezing it. "Maybe I could come back and visit you sometime, though." It had suddenly occurred to Katie that she might never see Lily again, and her heart dropped into her stomach.

"Absolutely," Nick said heartily. Too heartily. He was faking his enthusiasm, but Lily didn't seem to notice. The little girl leaned toward Katie and whispered, "Tell Mr. Snowman bye, 'kay?"

"You bet," Katie said, and taking Lily from Nick's arms, hugged her small body tightly while Nick moved Lily's and Helen's gear to the truck and spoke to her cousin.

Helen took Lily at last. "I guess I've been pretty rude to you," she said with a swift upward glance at Katie. "It's just that—"

"It's okay," Katie said. "Take good care of Lily. She's special."

Casting a swift glace at the plane, Helen's eyes then bored into Katie's. "Don't believe a thing that man tells you. He can't be trusted. He lies. He doesn't care about anyone but himself. Dump him at the police station and go back to your life."

Katie swallowed painfully. Of course, Helen didn't know about Katie's mom, abducted by strangers, abandoned by her husband, unwittingly trapped, awaiting help…or already dead. Katie said, "You'd better go." She kissed Lily one more time.

As Helen walked off with Lily, Katie stood by the plane. Nick said his final farewells and the truck took off. He stared after it for a long time and she fancied she knew a little of how he felt.

"So, now it's just the two of us," Katie said as he strode back toward her, straining to put a note of carefree humor in her voice to disguise her sudden sadness. She'd just lost Lily. In another hour or so, she'd lose Nick and be on her own with an injured man, trying to get him to tell her something she could use. There was also the nature of his injury to consider. A gunshot wound had to be reported to the police and Bill had panicked at the mention of police. Even more alarming, Nick had agreed with his father.

Did her mother's life depend on stealth and subterfuge? Might notifying the police be as dangerous as Nick's father believed? By trying to do the right thing, would she inadvertently do the wrong thing and how was she to know the difference?

And then there was Nick himself to consider. Approaching in that no-nonsense way he had, he returned her halfhearted smile. She couldn't help wishing she could tug him close and ease the melancholy from his eyes, that she could offer comfort and give it as well. This wasn't the time for romance, but romance was exactly the emotion that bubbled to the surface when Katie allowed herself to be open to what she was feeling. She couldn't help but recall the times their lips had touched, the way his gaze had delved deep and long into her eyes, as though he couldn't quite believe she was standing there, as though he wanted to know more about her, about himself…

"You, me and the Snowman," Nick said.

"Speaking of Mr. Snowman," she said, pushing dreamy notions aside and concentrating on reality, "I have something to tell you."

"We'll talk when we get back in the plane," he said, taking her arm, his breath a frosty halo around his handsome face. "Or haven't you noticed it's freezing out here."

AS NICK HELPED Katie climb back in the plane, he wasn't sure what course of action to take. He hated indecision. It cost lives in time of war. It moved nothing forward and the argument that at least it didn't make things worse didn't make sense to him. How could doing nothing ever make sense?

It was obvious to him that Katie's leg had started bothering her again. No doubt the preceding few hours, to say nothing of the ordeal of the night before had caused her a great deal of pain. She never said a word, however, just gamely limped along and seemed to focus all her considerable energy on other people.

She'd been hit by a car bad enough to end up in a coma and this was only a couple of weeks ago? Hit-and-run, the same thing that had happened to Patricia, only the results for his late wife had been devastating.

Images like war scenes assaulted his brain. Patricia lying on the pavement, groceries spilled around her broken body, blood seeping across the newly painted white line that ran down the center of Frostbite's main street.

He'd been coming out of the hardware store and he'd seen the whole thing, including the back of the car no one could ever identify. Worse, he'd witnessed his father's first steps toward Patricia, and then his cowardly retreat.

His father left her there, not even knowing Nick was fighting his way through the gathering crowd.

Nick blinked a few times to clear his head. It was too late for Patricia. His concern now was Katie. She should be at home, recuperating, not gallivanting around making recovery more difficult. He had to think of a way to get her to sit tight and let him take care of things, because that's the decision he'd just reached.

He'd take care of things.

If he could figure out how.

It was down to the wire now. The nature

of his father's injury would necessitate the police being called in and if what his father said was true, police involvement might mean the end of the line for Caroline.

Katie seemed ready to go it alone. Why? All night she'd been hounding him for help and now, on the brink of getting it, she wanted him to drop her off and fly away?

He was glad Lily was safe with Helen.

They climbed into the back of the airplane and closed the door. The space was cramped and his father took up most of the floor, so they sat side by side in the back. "Okay," he said briskly. "What did you want to tell me?"

"Your father regained consciousness during the flight."

"Which is why you were out of your seat."

"Yes."

They both looked as one to the prone man at their feet, at his gray skin, his sunken cheeks. It was hard to believe he'd ever been able to mumble a word much less hold a conversation. "Did he talk about your mother?"

Katie's eyes looked stricken as she said, "According to him, she was kidnapped from their motel room, right out of their bed, somewhere near Seattle. They hit him on the head, threatened him. He left."

"What?"

"According to Bill, after they beat him up they threatened him and he left."

"My God. Who is 'they'?"

"I don't know."

"And he didn't call the police or anything?"

"Apparently not. Do you think they may be holding her for ransom? Do you think he was coming to you for help raising money?"

"I don't know," Nick said, his expression perplexed. "It seems unlikely considering… everything, but then again if he was desperate enough… Did he say anything about a ransom?"

"No. When he finally realized we were in a plane flying away from Frostbite he grew quite agitated. He said we had to turn and go back."

Nick looked startled. "Was he lucid?"

"I think so."

"He's feverish, though. He might be rambling."

"I'm not crazy," Bill whispered.

The whisper was like a shout in the small space, and both Katie and Nick immediately slid to the floor on either side of him. Nick had to twist and crunch his tall frame in order to fit.

"Why do you want to go back?" Nick insisted.

For a moment, Bill's fuzzy expression cleared and he swallowed painfully. He said, "Just trust me."

Two things struck Nick at the same time. The first came out of his mouth. "Trust you? Now, why in the world would I trust you?"

The second was that he'd said that same phrase, "Trust me," to Katie a couple of times.

"Go back…to your house," his father said.

Katie said, "Is it the boathouse, is that it? Is my mother there or…"

Bill raised a hand and Katie stopped talking. His eyes closing once again, he said, "No…no, she's not there. Not…in Alaska."

Nick glared at his father. "I'm not going anywhere, until you tell me who this Carson is and why he shot you. Have you been following Katie? Is that why you ended up at my house on the same day she did? I need the truth, damn you!"

Katie stared at him as though he'd just pushed the button to initiate a nuclear explosion. "Nick—" she cautioned.

But he was tired of tiptoeing around the facts with his evasive old man. He cut Katie a stern look, before staring at his father.

"Come on. You're playing with a woman's life."

"She's my…wife…"

"Yeah, well, we all know how much you treasure yours or anyone else's wife."

Bill turned his head away. For a second, Nick experienced the thrill of victory—he'd pierced his father's facade. The thrill quickly dissipated. He'd taken a cheap shot at a man whose cooperation was vital. His own bitterness had exploded out of him and now seemed to coat the inside of the plane like some toxic green goop.

"Nice going," Katie whispered.

He shrugged.

She leaned close to his dad. Nick heard a few sporadic words uttered in her soothing voice. "…love…sacrifice…" followed by something he didn't hear and then, "…he's her best chance."

A few moments passed in silence as Katie straightened up and cast Nick a fleeting look he couldn't decipher. Hopelessness, maybe? If she thought she could sweet-talk the old man the way she had him—

"I left something…something at your house," his father mumbled in his increasingly reedy voice.

"When? Yesterday?"

"No...no, two years," he said.

Nick swore under his breath. Bill had left town after Patricia's accident without ever coming back to the house. He'd left clothes, a shaving kit, books. That first night, coming home after she died, Nick had dumped everything his father left behind into a box and given it to charity the next day. If there had been something Bill wanted, it was too late now.

"What did you leave?"

"Doesn't matter," his father said. "Must go back—"

"You need a doctor," Katie said.

"Not now. Take me back. Please...before it's...it's too late."

Nick swore. He stared into his father's watery eyes and finally took a deep breath. "And whatever you left at my house will help us get Katie's mother back? You understand I got rid of your clothes—"

"Not clothes..." Bill said, wincing with pain. Then he once again drifted away.

Katie said, "Are we really going back?"

"Do you have a better idea?"

"But he said my mother wasn't in Alaska. Besides, he needs a doctor."

"I know. But your mother may have more urgent needs. We'll be back in Frostbite in an hour. We can get to the house, reclaim whatever it is he left, then be landing in Anchorage two hours after that. Or, even better, I have an old army buddy who can take care of my father and he's only a forty-minute flight away. It's in the wrong direction, that's why I didn't think of him before, but if we can bypass Anchorage and fly directly south towards Seattle—"

"Seattle? You?"

"Who else?" he said. "Anyway, my pal Doc owes me a favor. Might be time to call it in."

There were few other choices, at least as far as Nick was concerned. In a race to save his father or Katie's mother, the poor woman won hands down.

He refueled the plane and then he and Katie spent an uncomfortable half hour cleaning his father's wound and rebandaging it. Instead of morphine, Nick gave his dad oral pain medication. Katie had brought along a Thermos of hot soup and she helped his father drink quite a bit of it, coaxing and cajoling like a pro, her soothing voice and abundant compassion no doubt warming his father as much as the broth.

Nick watched all this from the corner of his eye, amazed at how good she was. He suspected it went deeper than her knowledge that her mother's survival hinged on his old man's survival. He thought it probably went against her nature to hate anyone, to be cruel to anything. Hadn't his own daughter sensed Katie's character immediately, responding to her like a starving pup to a bowl of warm milk?

Thoughts of Lily caused his stomach to clench, and he rewrapped the remainder of the sandwich Katie had produced from a red satchel, made from the pot roast leftovers.

"It's time we got going," he said. "Like Sam said, another storm is predicted for late this afternoon. We'll have to take off before it comes or we'll be stuck sitting it out."

Which begged the question, what were they going back for? There was no way his father was up to another snowmobile ride, so they had to get him to tell what to look for.

Of course, Nick hadn't forgotten the aborted ambush by the bridge and the fact that an unknown—Carson?—gunman was still on the loose, making a trip back to his house a dangerous proposition. He'd leave Katie in the plane with his father. He'd go it alone.

Katie sat in the co-pilot seat this time, seemingly agog at all the dials and switches. Or maybe it was more than that keeping her quiet. Maybe she was thinking about all the time that had gone by. Which begged the question—how much time had gone by?

"When did your mother disappear?" he asked, using the headphones they both wore. The cockpit of a small plane was a noisy place.

She turned to him, blue eyes wide. "I'm not sure. A week, maybe two or three, maybe less. Mom had been out of communication with Tess for quite some time, but we don't know how much of it was just honeymoon stuff and how much of it was…this. How about your father? How did he get to Frostbite the night of the storm? In the red-and-white plane? What will the pilot think when one of his passengers is missing and the other has a bullet hole? And Nick, who is Carson?"

Nick shook his head. "Lots of unanswered questions."

Next thing he knew, Katie had taken off the headphones and sidled between the two front seats. He glanced back in time to see her drop to her knees beside his father. It was on his mind to stop her when he came to his senses. What did they have to lose? The man certainly seemed more comfortable talking to Katie than he did to Nick. He kept his mind on the business of flying and left the business of witness interrogation to Katie.

His part would come later.

Chapter Ten

Katie knelt on the floor beside Bill, bathing his forehead in cool water she shook from a bottle onto a clean cloth. His fever had suddenly spiked. Once again, she found herself wishing Tess had been able to come north. It should be her kneeling here. Tess's head was filled with medical knowledge.

What was Katie's head filled with? How to make a dirty martini? How to pull a draft beer correctly? The merits of Buffalo wings over nachos? How to maximize the profit from the sale of alcohol to cover the rising cost of quality food?

Pretty useless stuff.

She'd never felt useless before. As a woman with an active imagination and big dreams, she'd always been able to do just about anything she set her mind to. She could rotate her own tires, install a water heater if she had to, con the rowdiest drunk out of his car keys.

But she didn't know what to do when a man had a bullet hole in his chest or when another man was afraid of losing his daughter or when her mother—and the answers to all the vital questions she and she alone could provide—was in jeopardy, kidnapped for some obscure reason. These things left Katie high and dry.

So she bathed Bill's forehead with a damp piece of cloth and tried to still his tossing and turning, listening to his ramblings, committing every word—at least those she could catch—to memory.

He said "Lily" so often it was obvious his granddaughter was on his mind. He also mentioned Katie's mother, Caroline. He talked about snow and bullets and trucks and hooded men, and then inevitably, back to Lily and increasingly of Patricia, too, and the pain in his voice mirrored the pain that had to be wracking his body.

But the thing he kept reiterating the most had to do with Nick's fireplace. Katie remembered it as a massive wall of big rocks, rough and uneven. Was one of the rocks a false face? Could Bill have chiseled a hiding spot during those long Alaskan summer days when Patricia dug in her garden, Helen cleaned the cabins and Nick flew the paying guests on photo shoots? Could there be something hidden behind that little wooden door, back where the wood supply was?

It was possible. She could see Bill assuring Patricia he'd just sit inside with Lily while she napped, reading a book, drinking a cup of coffee, no problem.

Katie tried her theory out on Bill, asking questions, listening carefully to nonsensical ramblings. He was incoherent and agitated and brought up new subjects like ledges and spies and emeralds—the list went on and made no sense. What kind of pill had Nick given him? Was it possible Bill was allergic to the drug?

In some odd way he reminded her of her father, a man with secrets, a man with ghosts. Lots and lots of ghosts.

By the time they got to Frostbite, it was early afternoon. Katie's leg throbbed with a vengeance. Had she reinjured it? Did it matter?

Nick landed the plane with ease. Apparently Sam had done some runway clearing while they were gone. After they rolled to a stop by Nick's hangar and Nick turned off the engine, he turned to look over the seat at Katie.

"How is he?"

"Finally asleep."

"We'll have to wake him. I have no idea where to look and he can't make the trip on the snowmobile again in his condition."

"I don't think that's going to work. He's been literally unreachable since you medicated him."

"Great."

"I don't know if he's allergic to the medicine or simply getting worse. We need to get him to a doctor."

"And we will, but not before retrieving whatever it is he came for. I know you're anxious, I know you don't want to be here, but it has to be pretty important. I'm not leaving without at least trying."

"But how do we know what to look for? And how do we know there's even something still there?"

"Reading between the lines, my father made his way to Frostbite with, apparently, a killer. He risked all that to come to my place. If his was the face at the window that you saw last night, he probably saw me leave with Helen and knew I was gone. He checked, saw you and went away again. In other words, he wanted to get whatever it was he left and then disappear again without my knowledge. And that means, to me, that whatever it is he means to get must be a permanent part of my house, something not directly connected to him, something easy to take. He wouldn't count on my still having things he left behind over two years before."

She smiled. "It's as good a theory as any, I suppose."

He looked down at his father, who had mercifully stopped flailing and muttering and fallen into a very deep slumber. "Damn. Did he say anything at all that could help?"

"I have no idea. He talked about the fireplace a lot. Is it possible one of the rocks can be removed making a hiding spot?"

Nick seemed to consider this. "Offhand I'd say no, but it's someplace to start. We have three hours or so before we need to get the plane back into the sky. I'll be back by then."

"Wait a second, what do you mean *you'll* be back? Where will I be?"

"You'll stay here with…him. In his condition, who knows what he might do if he wakes up and finds himself alone? Or what if he says something important?"

"I'm not staying here," she said defiantly.

"Katie—"

"Listen, I could try to tell you everything he mumbled, but who knows if I'd remember it all? I need to go with you and see if something jumps out at me. He talked about ledges and emeralds and a bunch of other unrelated things. I can't do it from here. Isn't there someone else you could call to come stay with him? How about the guy who runs the airport. What's his name, Sam?"

"Sam's the salt of the earth, but he's also the biggest gossip in town. His wife isn't much better. No way I'm going to involve Helen's sister or Lloyd. Wait, there's Kitty. Damn, I should have thought of her before."

"Who is Kitty? How is she going to handle being asked to look after a man who should be on his way to an emergency room?"

"Like a pro. She's a retired air force nurse, and nothing fazes her except too much government and people with knives. I should have thought of asking her for help right at the start."

"Does she live close by?" Katie said, stuffing things back in her satchel. A sense of urgency filled her with a strange foreboding. Or maybe not so strange. Where was their erstwhile gunman?

"Not far," he said. "I'll get the plane back in the hangar and go fetch her."

CAROLINE MAYS—no, she reminded herself, she was married now, her name was Caroline Swope—spread one blanket on the cold earth and used the other to cover herself. She'd promised herself she wouldn't eat any of the food her abductors had left, but the promise hadn't lasted long.

The apple had been surprisingly good. Crisp—she hated soft apples. Cold. Maybe it helped that she was sitting in the dark with no distractions, but she thought not. If anything helped the apple taste better than normal, it was probably the thought that it might be the last apple she ever ate.

She'd cried for a while and been glad for the roll of toilet paper with which to blow her nose and dry her eyes. Now she was exhausted and wished with all her heart that she hadn't taken off her wristwatch before bed. She supposed she should be grateful she wasn't wearing one of the little flimsy nighties Bill favored and had insisted on cotton pajamas. They weren't exactly cozy, but they were better than half a yard of black nylon and a handful of lace.

She closed her eyes, her face resting on her hands so she could smell the good scent of apple instead of the musty smell of a grave. Her emerald wedding ring cut into her cheek, but she didn't mind. Almost immediately, her thoughts began to race back through time. She fought them at first, but then they seemed comfortable and safe and she allowed them to happen, allowed herself to spin lazily in their shadows. At first.

She was fifteen, pretty, popular, a good student. School was her sanctuary and she loved every moment she spent there mainly because it saved her from spending more minutes at home. Home was a nightmare. Her mother drowning in a bottle, the terror of her father's late-night visits to her bedroom, no one to listen to her, to help.

But school was safe.

And then when she was a sophomore, she met the buddy of a girlfriend's older brother, home from the navy, attending police academy. A good-looking man who made her feel unique and worldly and grown-up and safe. She married him when she was barely a junior, two months pregnant at the time, forging her parent's permission. She could still recall the gut-wrenching experience of leaving school and friends. Her new husband insisted they move away from the community. He had no family, no attachments and he didn't want anything to do with her family. Nor did she.

But, oh, the loneliness that followed as reality steadily ate away at fantasy. Her husband was sullen and moody. He gambled, kept secrets and ignored her, exacerbating every feeling of inadequacy she possessed. The days passed in long, unrelieved units she spent dreaming of the day her baby would arrive and she would at last experience the unconditional love and devotion she craved.

Caroline sat up with a start, hugging the blanket close, trembling from the inside out.

She couldn't do this. She couldn't sit here alone for days on end, not knowing where Bill was or what was going to happen or who those horrid men in hoods were, sitting by herself, thinking, remembering, regretting…she'd go mad!

She whispered, "Tess? Please, Tess, hear me. I need you."

The damp, cool earth absorbed her words like a sponge.

Caroline gave up trying to handle things like the forty-four-year-old woman she was and buried her face in her hands like a child.

NICK FOUND Kitty at home, curled up with a book. She agreed to help at once and was ready to go in minutes. The red-and-white airplane was still at the airfield and so Nick insisted on locking his plane in its hangar with Kitty and his father safely tucked inside.

Nick and Katie took one snowmobile and headed back to his place. Nick drove while Katie held on tight, wondering how he could still be alert enough to face the next few hours when he's had so little sleep the night before.

At least the snow predicted earlier in the day hadn't yet materialized. Once they left town, they took the logging road back toward the cabin, stopping when they reached the narrow bridge.

Nick turned the machine off, shed himself of his helmet and turning, faced Katie. She took off her helmet, as well, and for one fleeting moment, wondered what her hair looked like.

Nick removed his right glove and, reaching up, smoothed a tangle of bright red locks away from her face.

"I wish I had a picture of you," he said, his voice muffled by all the snow.

She smiled and, for a moment, allowed herself to lean into his warm hand. She closed her eyes, and the next thing she knew, his cool, dry lips touched hers.

Katie was no stranger to stolen kisses. But somehow this one was different. This man was different, and she didn't know if that portended well or poorly. It was no secret that she gave her heart too easily and that until now, it had been handed back in worse shape than when it left.

The kisses continued, so warm and so ex-hilarating in all the cold and haste and tension. She clung to him, half-tempted to lure him into the foliage and spread her coat on the snow. She wanted him closer, wanted his skin next to hers, and only the knowledge that this was hardly the time and place to begin an impulsive love affair kept her from whispering this idea into his ear. Still, it felt as though they were two shipwrecked sailors in a sea of white.

"My poor heart," she said at last, her head resting against his chest. He was wearing too many layers to detect a heartbeat though her fingers had stroked his throat a moment before and she'd felt a deep thump.

"What do you mean?" he whispered.

She glanced up at him. "Nick, you know how hopeless this is, don't you? You and me, I mean."

"I'm not thinking that far ahead," he said, kissing her forehead.

"You make me feel anything is possible, and that's a fantasy," she said, avoiding his gaze.

He chuckled. "Don't ruin a stolen moment in the snow," he said. "We've been shot at and lied to and said painful goodbyes and been scared. It's perfectly natural that we should find comfort this way."

"Now you sound like my high-school boyfriend," she said, sneaking a peak at his mouth. Big mistake. That mouth was made for kissing. Using a high falsetto voice, she mimicked the long-ago boyfriend. "Oh, Katie. Just one night, Katie, because who knows what will happen tomorrow. We could both be dead."

Nick smiled against her forehead. Imitating her pitch and cadence, he said, "Oh, Katie." He held her away from him and continued, his eyes as green as the snow-shrouded evergreen trees towering above them. "Just one night, Katie, because who knows what will happen tomorrow. We could both be dead."

They smiled at each other until the truth of this childish logic uttered under the present circumstances hit them both. Their smiles faded as their heads dipped together again, and this time the urgency behind his kisses had her heart pounding in her head until she all but threw herself off the snowmobile and took a few halting steps, regaining control as her feet sank into the deep snow.

When she looked back, Nick had unfastened from the snowmobile a pair of short skis.

"What are you doing?" she asked, turning. Using the same trenches she'd just carved, she returned to his side.

"The snowmobile is too loud," he said, strapping the skis onto his boots. "We can't

approach the house making all this racket—
we'll be sitting ducks."

"But I don't know how to cross-country
ski—"

"You couldn't do it anyway with that leg,
Katie. I'll go ahead and check things out,
then I'll send you a signal and you bring the
snowmobile." He unhooked two poles from
the vehicle.

"What kind of signal?"

He jerked his head back, indicating the
rifle slung over his back. "One shot followed
twenty counts later by one more shot. You
can still see the trail we made this morning,
you won't get lost."

Katie nodded. "Be careful—"

"If there isn't a second shot after the count
of twenty or if you don't hear anything at
all—or if you hear a volley, for that matter—
turn around and go back to Helen's sister's
house and get her and Lloyd to help you.
Don't come after me, Katie. My chances
will be better if you go get help."

She held up both hands as he got to his
feet. "Hey, I'm no heroine, you're on your
own."

"Promise me."

"I promise."

With a last, enigmatic look, he took off toward the house, the swish of his skis slicing through the snow, the only sound save the chattering of Katie's teeth.

She waited, growing colder as the shadows crept up the snowy, tree-lined lane and the sky darkened. She didn't think she could live in a place with so little light in the winter, even if the summers were long and pleasant. And she couldn't imagine Nick, who seemed totally at home with snow and all its trials, anywhere else.

Out of the blue, thoughts of Lily filled Katie's head. Was it possible she missed the little girl already? She tried to recall the tune the child had sung to her bunny. She tried to recall the story of the birdie and the palm tree. She was so damn cold, she tried to remember sitting underneath a palm tree, something she'd done once upon a time on a vacation to Florida when she was seven years old.

She glanced at her watch. Thirty minutes had passed.

Thirty-five minutes came, thirty-six minutes left. On the end of the current adventure, one had to add the time it would take to return to the plane and take Kitty home. No way around it, their window of opportunity was collapsing in on itself.

No signal. She'd promised to go get help.

Making one of her hasty decisions, she put on her helmet and climbed aboard the snowmobile.

She had a bad feeling…

She put the vehicle in gear and headed toward the cabin. She still had the handgun in her pocket. Nick must be in trouble.

She headed toward Nick.

Chapter Eleven

Katie decided she didn't have the strength, the stamina or the know-how to be subtle. She'd be the cavalry rushing in to help, damn the consequences.

And try not to make things worse.

Still, she wasn't crazy enough to ride to the rescue in such a way that she made an easy target, and so when she drew even with the boathouse, she stopped the snowmobile and parked it against the side, out of the way and hopefully out of sight of the house.

Taking off her helmet, she waited, listening, and when she heard no sound, took a few tentative steps forward.

She could see the ski tracks Nick had made. They led to the back door. Nick's skis and poles sat abandoned next to the door which, she finally noticed, was ajar. Footsteps led around the house. Caught in indecision about whether she should go inside the house or follow the footsteps to the front, she strained to hear something…anything.

What she heard was a gunshot. For a second, she actually counted to see if another shot was forthcoming. And then she heard a motor start at the front of the house. She entered the mudroom and ran through the kitchen and living room, toward the open front door, where she hurried outside and damn near tripped over Nick's prone form.

He raised his hands and shouted. "Don't shoot. For God's sake, Katie, put the gun down!"

Katie didn't remember drawing the gun. Breathing heavily, she looked toward the yard. A bundled-up shape riding a snowmobile was darting between the guest cabins, headed for the front bridge and the road beyond.

She considered firing, but by now he was too far away.

She put the gun down on the porch as she kneeled beside Nick.

"What happened to you?"

"I got hit on the head," Nick said, rubbing the crown of his head. "Thankfully, I was wearing my hat."

"I thought he shot you," Katie cried, helping him stand. "Was it the man your father called Carson?"

"I think so," Nick said. "He was limping and there was a bloodstained cloth wrapped around his thigh."

"Good."

"He looked into her eyes and added, "What are you doing here? You promised me you wouldn't come alone."

"I know. I'm sorry. I had a feeling."

"So you charged in here—"

"And saved you. Yes."

"You didn't save me."

"Of course I did. He heard the sound of my snowmobile—"

"No, he heard me trying to get in the front door."

"Whatever. Tell me what happened."

Taking off his knit hat and rubbing his head, he said, "I came in through the back and heard someone ransacking the living room. I went back out the way I'd come and snuck around to the front. I just had my hand on the doorknob when the door flew open. The guy was ready for me. He leveled his gun. I knocked it out of his hand as he fired. He hit me with the butt and the next thing I knew you were here and he got away."

"I wonder why he didn't stick around long enough to kill you?"

"Maybe he didn't find what he was looking for," Nick said, pulling his hat back on. "Maybe he's hoping I'll have better luck finding whatever it is we're all looking for and then he can bop me on the head again and steal it. Did you notice the condition of the house?"

"I was focused on the open door," she admitted. "Why?"

"You'll see." He gestured toward the still-open front door. "Take a look."

She walked back into the living room and stood for a moment absorbing things.

"You've been searched," she said.

"Big time."

The room had been turned upside down. Every cushion slit open, every drawer over-turned, photographic equipment and computer smashed. All of Nick's late wife's paintings had been torn from the walls, some slashed, most wrenched from their frames. Photos of Lily had been stripped from the walls, the logs stacked on the hearth thrown to the floor, the little door on the hearth wide-open, rugs rolled, books plucked from their shelves, CDs and DVDs, lying outside their crushed cases. The room, in utter chaos, was so cold their breath condensed.

"Oh, Nick. I'm sorry. I guess we're too late," Katie said.

Nick picked up the photo of Patricia and Lily and propped it back on the mantel. "I don't think Carson found what he wanted," he said. "He was making a hell of a lot of noise when I came in the back door. He wasn't done yet. He must have heard me. Help me check the rest of the house. I know he hadn't reached the kitchen yet."

They searched the other rooms and met back in the living room. "Nothing," Katie said.

"And so much in here. Makes you think that he somehow knew whatever he wanted was in this room."

They both looked at the devastation.

"Try prying the rocks from the fireplace," Katie said. "It would have to be a pretty tight fit, but maybe what we're looking for is a small bag of emeralds." As Nick found a screwdriver and started chipping away at the cement grout between the rocks, Katie shifted through some of the debris.

"Some of this just seems destructive for its own sake," she said. "The CDs and DVDs for instance. Why would anyone open every single case and dump out the contents? That was time-consuming and—"

"I bet we're looking for a disk of some kind," Nick interrupted.

"That makes sense. Some kind of information on a disk. Any luck with the fireplace?"

"Not so far. Tell me what else you remember my father mumbling about."

"Okay, let's see. Lily. Patricia. Emeralds. Cooking. Ledges. The fireplace. I can't think of anything else." She stared at the wood door. "What about that little door? Could he have hidden something inside there?"

He shook his head. "It leads to the wood supply. I've filled and emptied it dozens of times since my father was here."

"Have you ever taken a flashlight and examined up inside like on the ceiling?" she persisted.

He took his flashlight. Head and shoulders disappearing inside the small wood storage unit, he flashed the light all around the space as Katie peered over his shoulder. The small area was low on wood so the corners were easily visible. There was no handy little hiding spot. "Where does that door lead?" she insisted, pointing at a small door on the opposite wall.

"To the wood supply. It's a locked shed because of its access to the house. Give it up, Katie."

"Okay, I was wrong," Katie said, moving to Patricia's paintings as Nick closed the wooden door and went back to prying rocks. She stacked the paintings, careful to avoid the broken glass, trying to protect the paper. It looked to her like most of them could be reframed and saved. She found no hiding spot for a disk but tears flooded Katie's eyes as she thought of the legacy Nick's wife had left for her daughter.

And how some stranger had tried to destroy it.

Nick was suddenly at her elbow, pressing a tissue into her hands. "Leave them," he said.

"But it's her legacy—"

"Her legacy is Lily's goofy sense of humor. Lily's trusting nature, her hair and her chin. Patricia's legacy can't be destroyed this easily."

Katie wiped her eyes. For the first time

since meeting Nick, she felt a tinge of jealousy—for a dead woman. Nick's wife had accomplished a lot in her life, cut short though it was. "How old was Patricia when she died?"

Nick sighed deeply. Looking around his destroyed house, he said, "Twenty-eight. See that picture? That's the last one I have of her and Lily. It was taken the summer my father visited. Two weeks before…before she died."

"It's a beautiful frame."

"Yes. My father took the photo and had it framed. I've loved it despite—"

Nick stopped talking as he stared at the photo. When he started stepping over the mess to make his way to it, Katie followed. He'd picked it up by the time she got there and was turning it over in his hands. The glass front was cracked, but the frame had held together very well.

Katie said, "You don't think—"

"I don't know." Nick slid the levers that held the glass and photo in place, sliding out the cardboard backing and the photo itself so that all that was left was the cracked glass and the frame.

"The cardboard backing is kind of thick,"

Katie said. They took everything into the kitchen and set it on the table. The light was better in this room.

"Look at the edging around the cardboard," Katie said. "What if it isn't edging but a means of holding two separate pieces together?"

"With a disk hidden inside," Nick said. He produced a pocketknife and carefully slit the edge of the cardboard lining. With a gentle shake, an unlabeled CD fell onto the table.

Their success had happened so quickly that for a moment neither could believe it.

"I was sure it was emeralds," Katie said.

"Maybe it is," Nick commented as he slid the disk into his pocket. "But we're running out of time and the computer is trashed. Let's get back to the airstrip. My father has some explaining to do."

THE EARLY TWILIGHT hours approached as Nick opened the hangar door and parked the snowmobile outside, ready to give Kitty a ride back to her house. They'd seen no sign of Carson.

Anxious to see if his father had rallied under Kitty's care, Nick was still chagrined he'd not thought of getting Kitty involved earlier on. His conscious mind offered as reasonable excuses the unknown gunman, the cut telephone wires, the impossibility of leaving the house until their headlong flight to get his father away from Frostbite. To get Lily away, to get Katie away, and Helen. All decent explanations for such an obvious oversight.

But were there deeper reasons he didn't want to face?

Did it matter?

Bill was still feverish but he had a touch more color in his face. Kitty, a woman somewhere in her early sixties with silky white hair and blue eyes that never missed a thing, had taken expert care of the wound and delivered the proper pain medication. Kitty wouldn't accept a penny for her help, but Nick knew her house was always in need of some kind of maintenance. In a small and relatively secluded town like Frostbite, a lot of business was conducted on the barter system.

Nick gave Kitty a ride on the snowmobile, and stayed long enough for her to scold him for dillydallying around while the wounded man deteriorated. With dire threats delivered in her no-nonsense manner, she ordered him to get the man to a doctor post-haste before the infection spread.

She didn't ask who the stranger was or how he came to be shot or why they'd asked her to take notes of anything he mumbled. She didn't ask who Katie was or why Katie and Nick were both armed or what had happened to Lily. Nick thought her one of the least curious and most dependable people he'd ever met. And she reported his father hadn't said a single intelligible word.

He got back to the hangar in time to see the first snowflakes of a new storm approaching. In record-breaking time, he got the plane out of the hangar and onto the runway, refueled and checked out and ready to go. He didn't mention to Katie that the red-and-white plane was gone.

Katie stayed inside the plane with his father, bathing his forehead, listening for him to say something that would help.

"We're flying off into the wild blue yonder," Nick said, once the plane left the ground, "and besides knowing we have to get my father to Doc, I don't have the slightest idea what to do next."

Katie was leaning over the seat, her face close to his so she could hear him. How she managed to smell so good after the hours they'd spent traveling back and forth was a wonder to him.

She kissed his cheek and said, "You'll figure something out." Then she was gone, back to the rear of the plane, back to attend to his father, and he was left with a tingling sensation on his cheek that seemed to rattle what was left of his brain.

An hour later, after a brief conversation with Doc over the plane radio, Nick landed in an abandoned field next to Doc's house. Like many people who lived in remote areas, Doc had his own plane, and Nick rolled to a stop close by.

As Nick cut the engine, lights flashed on in an outbuilding. Nick slid into the back of the plane and opened the side door.

"Where am I?" his old man said, apparently rallying at the influx of cold air. His pupils were dilated, his expression blank.

"Somewhere safe," Katie said.

"Go back," he said. "Back to Nick's house."

Encouraged to hear his old man sounding more or less lucid, Nick dug the disk out of his pocket. "Been there and done that. We found it."

Bill zeroed in on the disk. "Thank the Lord," he mumbled.

"Quick, before we have to leave you here for medical help, answer a few questions."

"No police. No doctors—"

"Nothing official, not yet. Try to tell us something that will help find Katie's mother. Frankly, if you won't or can't, we'll have no option but to contact the police. We can't fly around forever."

"Yes, yes, okay," his father said, apparently sensing the urgency behind Nick's words. "How long—"

"You were shot less than twenty-four hours ago. How long have they had Caroline?"

He seemed to be searching his mind, adding and subtracting time. "Four days," he said at last, catching a sob in his throat. Even Nick was moved to a few pangs of pity for the guy. Katie looked ready to explode with emotion.

"Okay. What's on the disk?"

"Money. My life's savings."

"How much?"

"Over a million," he gasped, shivering now. Katie took off her coat and spread it over his father. She trembled from head to toe and Nick handed her a blanket. "It's in an account in the Bahamas," his father continued. "The information, it's on the disk."

"Where did you get that kind of money?"

His father closed his eyes and Nick swore under his breath. Looking up, he could see more lights coming from the outbuilding. Doc had said he'd bring his ATV out to the plane to collect Nick's father. Time was running short.

"You stole it, didn't you?" Nick said.

It took a moment for his father to utter one word. "Embezzled."

"Damn you!" Nick shouted, whirling out of control. His father had embezzled money and brought it, more or less, to his house, jeopardizing his family? He would gladly have throttled him in that instant, damn the consequences.

"Why did you bring it to my house?" he demanded. "What made you think I'd have let you through the front door if I'd known you were a thief? For God's sake, just who did you embezzle it from?"

Katie said, "Nick—"

He turned on her. "He's been an out-of-work alcoholic for half his life, Katie." Turning back to his father, he added,

"Who'd hire you? Come on, we don't have much time. Stop making me pull every piece of information out of you."

"Maybe if you stopped shouting at him, he'd give you answers," Katie said.

Nick swallowed deeply. She had a point. He said, "Carson followed you to my house?"

Bill looked away as he nodded.

Suspicion flooded Nick. The old man was hiding something. Probably the fact that he'd allowed himself to be brought here by Carson instead of refusing to talk and thereby protecting Nick and Lily. The man was a coward, but that wasn't news. Nick said, "Why did he shoot you before you collected the money?"

"I…I got away. I guess he figured he didn't need me to reclaim the money."

"So it's his money? It belongs to Carson?"

"No," his father said, still mincing words.

Anger came back in a flash. Nick stalked away from the plane, too upset to think clearly.

The next thing he knew, Katie, huddled in her blanket, was at his side. "You have to keep your temper," she said softly.

He stared down at her upturned face.

Though it was dark, he knew her features and could easily imagine the expression of concern she currently wore. He said, "I'm trying. He's still beating around the bush, keeping little secrets. For God's sake, the man is half-dead and he still can't just tell the truth."

She took his arm and led him back to the plane, talking quickly as they moved. "Listen," she said. "I had a father who lived a life of lies, too. Addictions, sneaking around, all of it. He never told anyone any more than he thought they needed to know. Habits like that die hard, Nick."

He stared at the ATV lights drawing nearer and said, "I guess. Listen, you take the lead, you talk with him."

"But you're his son—"

"Yeah, but you're the one who dispenses booze and advice in equal measure, remember? He knows I hate him. You talk to him."

She nodded. A moment later, they'd both climbed aboard. She immediately knelt by his dad and resumed bathing his brow. "Bill?" she crooned.

His old man's eyes flashed open immediately.

"Bill, you must love my mother. You just

married her. My sister said she is head-over-heels for you."

He didn't answer, but she sure had his attention.

"Nick can save her," she continued. "I don't know how. But Nick does. He can fix anything."

Nick half smiled at Katie's flattering words. He hoped she was right.

Staring into Katie's eyes, his father started talking again, his voice slurred, his words spaced far apart. The two small headlights of Doc's ATV bobbed over the light covering of snow outside, getting closer.

"I was an…accountant," his father mumbled.

People trusted him with their money? Nick shook his head. Unbelievable. Katie seemed to sense what he was thinking and he caught her glowering at him. She said, "Go on."

"I…my boss was…was laundering money." Bill's eyes kind of glazed over as he added, "So much money."

Nick heard himself snarl. "So you stole it."

"It wasn't theirs…either," Bill said, and focusing on Katie, added, "He was into…other things…worse things. It…it got to me. Had to…had to do…*something*."

"What did you do?" she coaxed.

"I knew someone…in…in the justice department. I was willing…I wanted…to turn state's evidence. Give back the money. All I wanted was…safety…protection…another chance…"

"And did they offer it?" Katie asked.

"Made me a…deal. Strapped wires on me…told me what to say. More evidence, new identity. Never had a chance. One of the cops…tried to kill me. He was in on it! I ran away but…nowhere to go. Knew Nick was in Alaska and I thought maybe…maybe if I gave him the money, he'd…he'd forgive me."

Bill was still addressing his comments to Katie. Nick clenched his jaw. So his old man had thought he could buy his way back into his only son's life?

"But you didn't give it to him," Katie said.

"He wouldn't talk to me," Bill said, and suddenly, though still halting, his voice took on a new strength. "Patricia, though…such a sweet girl. I hid the money away in the Bahamas…put the information on a disk. I taped the disk inside the photo I took of

Patricia and Lily. Good, solid frame. I was going to tell…Nick but…no time. Patricia…died…I ran…I ran…couldn't face Nick."

Nick closed his eyes and counted to ten as his father droned on, his voice growing increasingly anxious. "I wrote Nick…I tried…cop's name is Carson."

As Katie gasped, Nick said, "The man who shot you? The one who tried to blow us up? He's a cop?"

"Cop gone bad. He followed me here… He won't stop until he kills me…me and maybe you…we're all in danger." He licked his lips and his expression grew horrified. "My God, where's Lily?"

"It's okay, she's safe," Katie said. "But I don't understand. I thought you told Nick that Carson didn't take my mother. If not him—"

"My old boss. Benito Mutzi."

"The one you were an accountant for? The one you stole money from? He came all the way from New Jersey to Washington state to kidnap your wife, two years after you robbed him?"

"Time makes no…no difference to Benito…long memory."

Nick glared at his father and said,

"You're talking about the mob? You stole from the mob!"

Katie's hands flew to cover her mouth as she cried out. "The mob has my mother?"

"I took...something else...something more important than money."

Katie's brow wrinkled. "More? You took more what?"

"A kind of life-insurance policy. Hid it."

"Where?" Katie snapped.

"Seattle, two years ago." His eyes closed as a spasm of pain wracked his weakened body. He coughed. Nick was afraid they were about to lose him to unconsciousness.

Katie raised her voice as the same thought obviously crossed her mind. "Bill? Bill, stay with me! Tell us where you hid this life-insurance policy. Tell us what to look for. Bill!"

They held their breath as Nick's old man finally recovered enough strength to cry out, "Thumbnails," before breaking into silent tears.

Katie looked at Nick, questions burning behind her blue gaze. He had no idea what thumbnails meant. He said, "What else, Dad?"

It was the first time in memory that Nick

had used that term to address his father. It seemed to penetrate the fog of his father's feverish brain. He opened his eyes again. "Emerald," he whispered, licking his lips. "Find the star, find the…photo and the ledge…"

His voice trailed off. Nick said, "Wait. If I find these things, what do I do then? How do I contact Benito to get Katie's mom back?"

"Number in my pocket," his father said. He suddenly gripped Katie's wrist. "Tell her I'm sorry. Tell her I love her. Get the star…"

Katie and Nick had both bent over Bill as they tried to make sense out of his seemingly unrelated words. When his hand slipped from Katie's wrist and his expression grew slack, they looked at each other.

"Bill?" Katie said, turning again to Nick's dad. She felt his forehead before glancing back at Nick. "He's burning up. He has to tell us more, though. Wake him up. Get Doc to wake him up!"

"Calm down," he said, grasping her hands. "We have to keep him alive to get more answers, right?" He glanced out to see that Doc had made it to the plane. Two or three large dogs cavorted in the snow around Doc. Nick waved to signal just a moment.

His father coughed, a deep rattling cough that contorted his face. Nick gently searched his father's pockets until he found a folded strip of paper with a phone number scratched on it. "This is our only link to your mother," he said, tucking the paper into his own wallet.

"And our only link to the mob," Katie added with a shudder. "A murdering cop and the mob. How do we make a deal with the mob? How do we ever outrun them or outsmart them—"

Nick cupped her chin and tilted her face up to his. "Don't look too far ahead," he cautioned. "Take one thing at a time. Let's get him out of here."

With Doc's help, they managed to get the makeshift stretcher and its human cargo out of the plane without disaster and perch it across the back of the ATV. Seeing the way Katie limped, Nick insisted she drive while he and Doc walked alongside, balancing the stretcher. Doc told Katie to follow his tracks in the snow back to his house. The biggest problem was keeping out of the dogs' way as they circled the ATV.

They took Nick's father to a back bedroom made warm with an oil-burning furnace. Doc immediately went to work while Nick and Katie stood by the door and watched.

Doc was a few years older than Nick, another veteran of the Gulf War, a doctor who had long lived in his Alaska home situated on a large parcel of land in a place so remote it didn't even have a name. He lived with three German shepherds and a white cat who currently sat on a wicker chair near the bed staring at Nick's father.

Doc wore his graying hair in a long ponytail almost as skimpy as his beard. Only the very bright blue of his eyes suggested an active intelligence. Otherwise, he looked as though he'd spent the past few years sleeping on a park bench.

"He'll pull through," Doc said after a quick examination. "I'll start an IV drip to rehydrate him and get the right drugs started. I'll clean up the shoulder. His heart doesn't sound good though, folks. Sounds like a mitral valve problem. You know anything about that?"

"Nothing," Nick admitted.

"Me neither," Katie said, voice shaky.

"My cell phone still can't pick up a signal. If you have a phone, I could call my sister and she might know something."

"No phone, but there's a shortwave radio that should work. Nick can help you use it," Doc said.

Nick had been hoping the cold trip on the ATV along with the barking of the dogs would rouse his father for one more conversation. A few details, for instance, would be nice. What exactly constituted a life-insurance policy for a man like his father? Where had he hidden whatever it was? And what did he mean he'd been followed when he left?

Nick glanced down at Katie. He wanted her to stay here with Doc while he went to Seattle. He didn't want her involved with mobsters and a cop gone bad. How to convince her? He tried a couple of approaches in his head, but neither one stirred the imagination or, he suspected, would get results. Her blue eyes staring into his made rational thought tricky.

"Don't even think of trying to leave me behind," she said, proving once again she was a mind reader. He hoped that was all she could read of his mind. "You're going to need all the help you can get. I'm going with you."

"But—"

"I promised Tess I would bring Mom back alive and well and bursting at the seams to explain all this to us, and that's what I plan to do."

"But—"

"Anyway, you're a little rusty when it comes to playing nice with other people."

"Do you think I plan on playing nice with the damn mob?" he snapped, finally getting in a word or two.

He was instantly sorry he'd said it. "No," she said, blue eyes glittering, "I am not expecting you to play nice with the damn mob. But we're a team now. Lopsided, sure. But a team."

He smiled faintly. Some team. A burned-out ex-soldier and a bartender.

"You watch, you'll find you can't live without me."

And that, in a nutshell, was what he feared most.

Chapter Twelve

Nick used the shortwave to contact a man he knew in San Francisco who then used his phone to call Tess and ask a few questions.

Katie had been disappointed to find she couldn't just call the hospital. She really wanted to hear Tess's voice and ask her advice. Though they'd had little chance to actually be twins, having only known of each other's existence for a week, Katie found the mere thought of having a sister fortifying. It was like having someone to cover her back, someone who would be there forever.

Men came and went. Men loved you and then they didn't. Even fathers had a terrible tendency to wander off, and she'd never experienced having a mother, at least not that she could actually recall. But a sister. A twin sister, that was different.

What she got instead was a call back on the radio, but it wasn't from Nick's old friend. Instead Ryan Hill, the cop who had been her father's partner and was now engaged to Tess, had found a radio of his own. He and Katie held the stilted conversation indicative of taking turns talking and remembering to say "over and out" when finished.

But at least Katie now knew that Tess was slowly recovering. Plus, she could hear the love in Ryan's voice as he talked about Tess. She'd known Ryan for years and never had second thoughts about him—cute, sure, but not her type. She didn't want to spend the rest of her life with a cop. Dad had been enough. But Ryan was Tess's dream man and in Katie's book, that made him ideal…for Tess. If he ever hurt her…

Well, that was just borrowing trouble.

The other reason Katie wanted to talk to Tess had to do with money. Fuel for the plane, Seattle, food, whatever—she couldn't go on depending on Nick to pay for everything, and yet she felt very uncomfortable using Tess's charge card. She'd always paid her own way in life and all this taking was getting on her nerves.

There was nothing to be done about that, however. She would have to settle it all in the future. Somehow.

It was Nick's turn next. He called Helen, whose cousin had a shortwave in her house. When he asked to talk to Lily, Katie sat forward, shamelessly eavesdropping. The conversation was full of laughter and inane comments that sounded warm and comforting. Daddy-speak.

Back on the radio with Helen, Nick asked her to call the Juneau airport and make two reservations on a commercial airline for the next morning. This was the first time Katie had heard of this plan—she'd assumed they'd fly back in Nick's plane. He also told Helen a little of what was going on and Katie could easily imagine the scowl on Helen's pale face as she read between the lines. The conversation ended with a warning: his house had been searched and she shouldn't go back to it, especially not alone.

Did Nick feel a million miles away from those he loved, those who depended on him? His connection to his family and a single location on the earth awakened in Katie a sense of loss. Though she'd spent most of her life in New Harbor, her father was now dead and her friends had scattered. She'd been directionless so much of her life. She felt a new need to dedicate herself to something important. She wasn't a child anymore.

After the calls, Katie and Nick sat down with mugs of stew and crispy bread, a piece of paper between them. Doc had taken his mug to the sickroom. Tess hadn't known any more about Bill's heart condition than they did and Doc was worried about his only patient. The cat went with Doc while the three big dogs curled up on a rug before the fire and watched Katie and Nick eat.

Doc's cabin was a fraction the size of Nick's log house. It seemed to consist of two bedrooms, a pocket kitchen/living area combination, and a couple of small ante rooms like the one that held the radio equipment. It was stuffed with too much mismatched furniture but that gave it an eclectic, cozy feel, heightened on a cold night with the oil burners and a fireplace and the good smells of home cooking.

"I didn't know about your plan to take a commercial flight to Seattle," Katie said between mouthfuls of the wonderful stew.

"It's the fastest way," Nick said, offering her a piece of bread.

"I take it we fly from here to Juneau?"

"We'll leave early in the morning," he said. "Should take us four hours to fly to Juneau, then we'll board a commercial plane. The flight to Seattle will take two-and-a-half hours. Main benefit is we won't have to land to refuel in Canada."

"What's wrong with Canada?"

He looked into her eyes. His looked tired and discouraged. "I need to take a gun, Katie. Canada frowns on that. We'll pack it in my suitcase and check it aboard. We'll leave yours here."

Katie's spoon clattered against the pottery bowl as she dropped it. Tears gathered behind her nose and she shivered. The reality of the situation hit home with a bang as she thought about what lay ahead. Nick at risk, Lily fatherless as well as motherless…the possibilities of loss staggered her.

Nick reached across the small table and touched her hair. "It's okay, Katie."

"I'm scared," she said.

"Your mother—"

"I'm scared for you, Nick. Take me to

Juneau, then go collect Lily and go home where you're safe."

"The little lady has a point," Doc said. He'd approached without being noticed and now leaned against the door jamb, his empty mug cradled in his hands. "You've fought enough battles, amigo," he added.

Nick laughed. The sound was unexpected. Doc shook his head while Katie stared at Nick. "Doc, you know me better than to think I'd walk away now. And Katie, what exactly would you do by yourself in Seattle?"

"Call the police," she said.

"That's what I thought. You're not used to these kind of people. They won't hesitate to cut your mother's throat. It's written on the paper I took from my father's pocket that he has a week to call the phone number they gave him. Seven days."

Katie's jaw dropped. "A week? I didn't know that."

"I didn't tell you. But this is day four. Maybe day five. We don't have long. It's up to me…and you. We'll do what we have to do. Then we'll go back to our everyday lives."

She nodded.

"With a cruising speed of one hundred thirty-eight miles per hour and a maximum range of about four hundred fifty miles, it would take us almost two days of flying and stopping for fuel and shut-eye to get us to Seattle in my plane. We don't have that kind of time. We need to arrive tomorrow. We need to figure this thing out tomorrow. So, let's talk about what we know."

Doc shook his head again as he crossed to the sink to deposit his bowl. "Still crazy after all these years," Doc said.

"True. Hey, Doc, you have a computer? We have a disk that needs looking at."

"I don't have a computer or a television set or telephone. I have a heck of a wood shop and 2,003 books. I have peace and quiet on my terms."

"I should have known. Thanks anyway."

"While you guys figure out your problems, I'll stick close to your dad, Nick. If he regains consciousness, I'll tell you."

Nick nodded his thanks as Doc left the kitchen. Looking at Katie, Nick picked up the pencil and said, "What do we know?"

Katie took a deep breath, relieved the threatened tears had never spilled onto her cheeks. "Your dad embezzled over a million dollars from the mob," she said. "He went to the justice department for help and they offered him a new identity if he would allow himself to be wired and sent back in for more evidence. Before he could do that, one of the cops who apparently was assigned to help him tried to kill him."

"Carson. The man I shot."

"Right. So your dad put his money in an offshore bank account, but he didn't want it for himself, he wanted it for you. He came to Alaska and when you wouldn't have anything to do with him, he put the information on a disk and hid it in your house. Then Patricia was killed and he chickened out—"

"Again."

"Yes, again. He came south toward Seattle and apparently someone picked up his trail and started after him. He had taken the precaution of taking other evidence from his employer."

"And when he realized he was being followed, he hid what he had taken. That's the bargaining chip for your mother. His 'life-insurance policy.' That and the money. So what form did this life-insurance policy take? And where did he hide it?"

Katie nodded at the paper. "This is where

you make the list. Let's see. He's mentioned emeralds several times now. And a ledge. What ledge? He goes on about photos, but that's probably because that's where the disk was hidden in your house."

Nick wrote down the few meager words. "He mentioned water and clams, too."

"The beach?"

Nick shook his head. "This is impossible."

"No, it's not. Maybe your dad will talk more tonight. I'll sit up—"

"Doc won't allow that, Katie. He'll sit up."

She looked down the hall and said, "He's a nice man."

"Yeah. He's a good one. Just a little antisocial."

"Seems friendly enough to me."

"That's because you're with me. Doc and I go way back. I saved his life once. Come on, let's get some sleep."

Before they could go to bed, Doc asked Katie if he could examine her leg. She removed her boot and sock and pulled up the flared jeans, then unwound the elastic bandage. Her leg was still mottled with bruising. Doc said it would improve faster if she stopped walking on it so much, and sent her off to sleep in his room, refusing her offer to take a turn watching over Bill and all but forcing a pain reliever on her.

"Won't be the first night I stayed awake," he said as she swallowed the pill. "Won't be the last."

Nick was already in Doc's bed, piled beneath a mountain of old quilts, eyes closed. Katie turned off the light he'd left on for her and undressed in the dark, leaving on her underwear which had been chosen for warmth and not a sexy rendezvous, and then pulling back on her long-sleeve cotton T-shirt. She gingerly crawled into bed next to Nick, attempting not to disturb him.

The headache she'd suppressed all day with nothing more than determination thundered in her temples. Closing her eyes brought some relief. Come on, pain pill, she chanted, but soon realized it was more than the headache that had her flustered.

She was in bed with a man she found increasingly desirable.

Anxiety manifested itself in a bit of tossing and turning. His face was so close, his breathing so regular, his body heat seeped through the sheets, drawing her like a moth to a flame. He must harbor no feelings for her whatsoever to have fallen asleep instead of waiting for her to come to bed, and staying asleep once she wiggled beside him.

That was discouraging.

And then he caught hold of her hand and brought it to his lips, kissing her knuckles, folding her hand within his to rest against his bare chest. Fire leaped through her body at his touch and she inched closer.

"Your virtue is safe with me," he mumbled, "so stop fretting."

"That's not why I'm fretting," she whispered into the dark.

She felt his breath caress her cheek as he turned to face her. "I never know quite what to make of you," he said.

"What you see, or in this case don't see, is what you get," she said, wishing he would kiss her. She didn't want to make the first move, but then she wasn't proud....

"This isn't the time," he added.

"It isn't? And how do you know that?"

"I'm older and wiser. I know."

"You're full of it."

"You need someone with a heart to give,"

he said, his voice so soft she wondered if he was close to sleep.

"You have a heart," she said.

"A little one," he mumbled.

"No room in it for me?"

"Not the way you want. Not the way you deserve."

"And how do you know what I want or what I deserve?"

"Don't tempt me, Katie."

She turned her head away as two tears slid out of her eyes and onto the pillow. She left her hand cradled in his and she could tell by his breathing that he'd fallen asleep.

She'd been treating him like an ordinary man and he wasn't. Some code of honor had propelled him to agree to help her. But it wasn't affection for her; he wasn't doing this because she needed or wanted him to do it. He was honoring his family name, so to say. He was taking care of business his ne'er-do-well father began. Yes, he'd kissed her a couple of times, but so what? It had been an emotionally charged two days. She needed to back off and leave him alone to do what she couldn't do, couldn't even imagine how to do: find and save her mother.

Her mother, held for ransom with a group

of people infamous for their disregard of human life.

She closed her eyes again and breathed in the good, fresh smell of Nick's skin. She replayed his drowsy warning, but superimposed over it was the interlude in the trees when they'd stopped the snowmobile in the snowy lane and he'd turned and kissed her. The way he'd looked at her.

The urgency of his kisses.

Nick was two men. One wanting, one refusing. She considered shaking him awake.

Instead she fell asleep.

THE NEXT DAY BEGAN before dawn when Nick roused her with a quick, "It's time to get ready."

He was in the act of pulling on a sweater—a new one, undoubtedly belonging to Doc. She was about to comment on this when she saw her own suitcase on the dresser. Someone must have retrieved it from the plane before waking her.

Showered and wearing clean clothes, her hair freshly washed and still damp, a quick breakfast of scrambled eggs and toast in her stomach, she was ready to leave when Nick was. The plane was off the ground soon after.

"Let's use the flight to Juneau to review what we know about Carson."

Katie sat back in her seat and adjusted her headphones to a more comfortable position before saying, "Okay. There are two groups of bad guys, a cop named Carson and the mob. Carson wants your dad dead."

"And probably us as well."

"And the mob who have my poor mother hidden away somewhere. At least I hope they do. There's nothing to keep them from killing her, is there? I mean what would they have to lose?"

Nick put his hand on top of hers. She met his steady gaze and swallowed her panic. It wasn't fair to expect him to sweep up after her emotionally all the time. She said, "There I go again. I'm sorry."

"It's okay. Back to Carson—"

"He searched your house so he had to know something was there."

"I think my father bargained with Carson—the money for his life. Then my father must have escaped from Carson, Carson followed, decided the money was a ruse, shot my father, got wounded by me and fled."

"Then the next morning you blew up

Carson's snowmobile and we left. He decided he might as well search the house. I wonder where he got another snowmobile? He was riding it away from the house when I rescued you."

"You *rescued* me?"

"Don't quibble semantics. So, where did he get the other snowmobile?"

"He must have come across the one my father used to get to my house the night he was shot. They must have come together, more or less. We don't know if Carson left on that red-and-white plane or if he stayed in Frostbite in which case, he's no doubt in the process of destroying my house."

"At least we're not in it," Katie said softly.

The hours passed in a flash, both of them well rested and anxious about what was to come. Nick landed in Juneau at a water airport. There was no snow on the ground though it was raining steadily. They took a cab to the commercial airport, bought the tickets Helen had reserved in their names, went through the procedure of locking the gun in a suitcase and signing the proper forms, and were the last people to board the plane.

As soon as they were in the air, Katie

thought to ask Nick if Doc had mentioned Nick's father having any moments of lucidity during the night.

"Just one and it wasn't that lucid," Nick said. He reached in his pocket and took out a scrap of paper. "This is what Doc could make out of Dad's ramblings. 'Caroline, car chase, south, emeralds, nightgowns, wedding and clams.'"

"It sounds as though he's mixing his time periods. Two years ago with a few days ago," Katie said. "But some of those words are ones he repeats over and over again. They have to mean something."

"Yeah, but what? We'll rent a car—"

She put a hand on his arm. "About the money for all this," she said. "I don't have much of my own, but I do have my sister's credit card and there should still be a few hundred on it. I'll take care of the car and I'll repay you for fuel. I don't see how I can compensate you for your time."

"You can't," he said, looking into her eyes. "You can't afford me."

She narrowed her eyes. "How much do you charge?"

"By the week? Six thousand."

"Yikes."

"It's all-inclusive," he said. "Cameras if need be, flight time, food, entertainment, lodging...although in your case, we have to factor in my father. He got you and your mom into this so I figure a big discount is in order."

"Good. Let me know how much I owe you."

"I will," he said.

"I will repay you," she insisted.

"You can repay your half if you want." His face hardened as he added. "But not mine. You understand I'm here for reasons of my own, right?"

She understood.

Chapter Thirteen

The flashlight beam had grown increasingly weak until now its wavering beam glowed more yellow than white. Caroline was afraid to leave it on for very long. The thought of losing even that fledging bit of light made her throat constrict.

The hole in the ground hadn't improved, either. In fact, over the days it had become damper as though it had rained and the water had seeped into her cell. The floor wasn't exactly muddy, but it felt slimy and uncomfortable and sometimes she felt slippery things. Paying the price for a flash of light, she'd discovered worms. She wasn't alone anymore.

If she lived through this, she would never dig a hole and plant a flower again. Never.

One thing she knew. Bill was dead. He would have saved her from those men if he could have, her poor darling, and by now he'd had plenty of time to call the police. But hour after hour—day after day—passed without rescue and now she had to face the fact that none might ever come.

There was only one apple left, though she'd tried to eke them out. One. Did the number of apples signify anything important? Would someone come back and empty the bucket she had placed as far away as possible from where she sat and replace her food and give her new batteries?

Sure they would. Or maybe she should just ring for room service.

Where was she? Why could she hear almost nothing, even when she put her ear against the plywood roof or that little pipe of fresh air?

And why had this happened to her? Those men had broken into the room all of a sudden, bursting through the door like the vice squad. They'd dragged her and Bill out of bed, struck him on the head and stuck a cloth over her face. That was the last thing she recalled until waking up in this hole. If they hadn't murdered her outright, did that mean she was a hostage? And did that mean Bill was even now trying to dig up enough money to free her?

But Bill didn't have a lot of money. He did

the books for a dozen small businesses, but there was no money in that. She didn't have much either. And Tess? Maybe a little nest egg—the girl was a tireless worker and had a good job with a successful veterinarian practice—but enough to justify trying to extract a ransom for her mother?

No way.

Did Tess know about this? She and Bill had canceled their fancy room in Seattle, so did Tess just think they'd taken off for Canada or who knows where? Had her only child realized yet that her mother's honeymoon had turned into this nightmare?

Only child?

So, was this some kind of cosmic retribution for what she'd done when she was young? Was it payback time?

She closed her eyes, and this time when thoughts of the past crowded in on her, she had a plan. Why hadn't she thought of this before? Memories were selective; she didn't have to be their victim.

This realization was empowering. Yesterday or the day before, when she'd relived the shock of delivering twins and not the lone baby she'd so desired, she'd felt that old pain, that old guilt…

Why not just remember it differently? Remember it happy and relaxed, remember how she'd felt a sense of wholeness she'd never experienced before—

It was no use because none of that was true. It hadn't happened that way and pretending it had wouldn't work. The fact was the temporary awe of having two babies fled as reality reared its ugly head. Her marriage was a sham, and now there were two little individuals to look after. Not that they seemed to need much. They shared a crib, they shared coos and first smiles. She could tell when she was around them that they would cling to each other for the rest of their lives. They would nurture and love each other. Instead of creating one person in the world who would love her unconditionally, she'd created a self-sufficient duo. She would be the outsider. Forever.

The sense of betrayal. The doom. The guilt for having feelings so awful and self-centered.

Suddenly, she hadn't wanted either of them. Taking care of them became a nightmare. No one knew about postpartum depression then. No one had a nice name for it and caring doctors and medications. Once again, no one listened, no one helped, she was alone. A zombie. A failure. Scared.

She pushed the pain away. She had to. She closed her eyes and hummed, trying to relax in her cold, mucky hole, pulling the wool blankets tighter around her body. She'd erase her mind, make it blank, fill it with silly things like lyrics of songs or strings of numbers…

If madness lay in this direction, she was ready to embrace it. What did it matter?

THE PLANE LANDED south of Seattle at the Sea-Tac airport. It was almost noon and so foggy Nick was relieved not only that they were on the ground but that he hadn't been in the pilot's seat. Katie insisted on renting the car using her sister's credit card. He didn't argue. He understood her brand of independence and admired it. Instead he reclaimed their luggage, most importantly of all, his handgun.

Katie's presence delighted him more than he'd ever tell her. He'd told himself that since she was privy to the same information he was, and since she was as stubborn as they came, she'd no doubt follow him and become an additional liability if he sneaked off without her. But the truth was simpler. It had been a long time since he'd felt part of something bigger than himself. And she was right. He wasn't great with people.

What dangerous thoughts, he mused as she checked out the rental for any existing scrapes or dents. She was so young, she had a rich, full life ahead of her. Him? He'd had his rich, full life. It had died with Patricia, out on the street, and now he knew more about life and love and loss than Katie—hopefully—ever would.

Not that she hadn't had her fair share of drama for a woman her age. Not that at times she didn't seem wiser than he would ever be, but it was a wisdom based on fearless innocence and not experience.

Okay, he craved her. First woman since Patricia to create those tender feelings, to incite lust, to tease his senses. She was a treat to look at, a challenge to communicate with, frustrating and delightful. Her quirks ignited his imagination and the way she felt in his arms, pressed against his body, the feel of her warm lips was—well, it was kind of like coming home after a long, long absence.

It had cost him a lot to put her off the previous night and he blamed himself for her assumption he wanted more to happen. He shouldn't have kissed her even one time, let alone a dozen times. He shouldn't have flirted with her out in the snow with the towering trees like a cathedral above their heads, nerves honing every sensation. He'd been powerless to resist her chilled lips and porcelain skin, powerless to resist his longings.

Excuses.

Face it, her enthusiasm and passion were like a life force of their own. When she'd crawled into bed with him the night before, he'd had to remind himself she was also too precious to waste on an old fool like himself.

None of this mattered.

Time was running out.

Concentrate on the task at hand. Time for what-ifs and if-onlys later...

As he was more familiar with the city than she was, he did the driving. It was one in the afternoon by the time they took the exit to the waterfront which, they both decided given the mention of water and clams, was as good a place to start as any.

"Your dad's preoccupation with clams is an odd one," Katie mused as he dealt with the midday traffic.

"You should have asked Tess for the wedding-day menu. It could be as innocent as clam chowder," he said, cutting her a quick glance. She looked wonderful, glowing in a pink sweater, the red tresses falling around her delicate features, setting off the wild blue yonder of her eyes. She clasped her hands together tightly in her lap.

"Turn up the heater if you're cold," he told her.

"It's this fog," she said. He agreed. Chicago's fog might creep in on little cat feet, but Northwest fog oozed through the streets and hung over the water like an extra on a horror movie set.

"It seeps into your bones," Katie added. "And it looks to me as if it's getting worse instead of better."

"You're from the Oregon coast. You must have lots of experience with fog."

"Doesn't mean I like it," she grumbled. "Where did you grow up?"

"Born in New Jersey, moved to California when my mother remarried. We lived in Los Angeles. I'm more used to smog than fog."

"And this traffic doesn't faze you."

"Nope."

"And after Los Angeles," she said, turning

in her seat to watch him, "you joined the Army?"

"And went to war. Ex-Ranger," he added, though in his mind, that had all taken place at least two lifetimes ago.

Katie, who always appeared to be tuned into his thought processes in an alarmingly accurate way, said, "My dad used to say life was like a book with chapters. Childhood, coming-of-age, career, building a family, old age—he always urged me not to rush one stage along in order to get to the next stage faster."

"It's sounds to me like your father was a philosopher."

She was quiet for a second and then she said, "You know, I guess because Dad is dead and beyond questioning, my sister and I have blamed everything on my mother. How could she separate us and keep us apart? Could you have given away Lily's twin and sworn never to see or touch her again?"

He glanced at her as he merged lanes. "I don't think so. But everyone has different breaking points. Your mother must have been under considerable stress."

"Yeah. But I don't understand it."

"Katie, did you have a happy childhood?"

She pondered this for a moment before saying, "In many ways, yes. Dad was a good father, but he was fighting a gambling addiction so money was always tight and he was away a lot and I was on my own. I always knew something was wrong and, like kids do, I always felt it was somehow my fault. I think he loved me as much as he knew how."

"And I guess there are worse ways to grow up," Nick said.

"And better ways. I look at you with Lily and it just makes me smile inside."

She'd just managed to chip away another piece of his defenses. He'd told her last night that his heart was too small to hold her inside and it was true. He knew the stories about how love expanded a heart and there was always room for one more, but his was battle weary and ready for semiretirement. There was room for Lily. Acres of room for Lily. The rest of that precarious real estate had to be labeled off-limits, flood plane, earthquake zone, tsunami warning, bridge out ahead, no lifeguard on duty.

If Katie would stop being Katie, he could stop thinking about her. Since that seemed unlikely to happen, he would have to do the next best thing. He would have to solve this current situation posthaste and go home to Lily.

He said, "We were talking about the possibilities of the word 'clam.'"

She graciously accepted getting back on track. "Okay. Well, clam chowder, like you said. Clambake. Clam diggers. Clam up. Plain old clamshells."

"Piece of cake figuring out the right one," he said drily. They ended up driving along Puget Sound, the underpinning of a raised highway on one side, restaurants, gift stores and piers on the other. On this cold, late February afternoon, the tourists were few and far between and the scenery was distorted by the pea-soup fog.

"All this talk of clam chowder has made me hungry," Katie said. "Let's park and get something to eat."

Nick found a parking spot and they bundled back into their coats and scarves and gloves. The weird thing was that it was so much warmer here than Frostbite and yet the fog made it seem colder.

"The emerald thing," Katie said. "That has to be gemstones."

"Or maybe the color of your mother's eyes."

Katie stopped walking. "I don't know the color of my mother's eyes. I still haven't ever really seen her." She looped her arm through his and squeezed him. She was always doing little things like this. Warm things, friendly things, ordinary affectionate things. With a sigh he added, "Nightgowns and your mother's name, those seem obvious."

"Well, it was their honeymoon," she said, once again walking. "What about his reference to thumbnails? Torture?"

Nick had checked his father's thumbnails. They looked fine, which meant if anyone was being tortured it was Katie's mother and he didn't want her thinking about that. He said, "No idea."

"How about car chase?"

"Now that's interesting."

"Let's make a scenario. Say your father was coming south. Didn't he mention something about someone following him?"

"Like everything else, he said something and then failed to explain it." They crossed the busy street and began walking down the sidewalk, looking in at different restaurants. He'd leave the choice to her.

She said, "Okay. Say he figured out there

was someone trailing him. Say he still had whatever it was he stole from the mob." Her voice dropped dramatically as if she feared being overheard.

"I'm with you," he said.

She stopped walking and, turning to face him, gripped his arms with her hands. Looking up at him, she said, "So what if he came into Seattle knowing someone was following him and he wanted to lose them. He made his way down here and parked and disappeared into one of these stores or restaurants. It was summer—it would be a lot more crowded than it is today. The big public market is right up the hill. That place is a maze of flowers and fresh fruit and seafood and jewelry and heaven knows what else. Think about all the different levels, all the quirky corridors and twists and turns, all plugged with so many shoppers you can hardly see a foot in front of you. Dad used to take me there when I was a kid. Great place to get lost."

"Okay. Then what?"

"Then he got hungry and wanted something to eat," she said.

Playing along, he said, "There are dozens of places to eat in that market."

"Yes there are." She gazed behind him, biting her lip, concentrating. Then she smiled. "Or he could have walked down to this street."

"Why down here?"

"It's closer to the water? I don't know."

"Okay, *where* down here?"

She turned him around until he was looking at the restaurant she'd been facing. Bright green letters spelled out, *Emerald Water Fish Company...home of Seattle's best clam chowder!*

Speaking over his shoulder, she said, "Right in there."

"THIS IS DELICIOUS," Katie said, spooning the creamy chowder into her mouth.

Nick sat watching her, his own bowl empty. He said, "Okay, Sherlock, we found *emerald* and *clam* and even *water.* Now what?"

"Now we figure out where he would hide something in this restaurant."

Nick looked around them. Again, given the off season and the in-between mealtime hour, the restaurant wasn't terribly crowded, but on a summer day two years ago? It was a large room with wood-plank floors, round tables with captain chairs and windows surrounding three sides. A bar ran along an interior wall. Every inch of wall space was covered with some sort of nautical memorabilia or framed photos of fishing boats hauling aboard huge catches. There were a million places to slip something, but now that they seemed to have identified the meaning of *emerald* in his father's rambling words, exactly what kind of treasure were they actually looking for?

Gemstones? Something green?

Katie said, "I found the restaurant. You find the… whatever."

He sat back in his chair as she crunched into a slice of garlic toast. "Okay, let's see. Assuming that he stashed it here and assuming it's still here after two years, it has to be somewhere not likely to be spotted and that means in or on or behind something prominent—remember, he didn't have long to figure this out—and permanent."

A waitress stopped to refill his coffee cup and, after he thanked her, he said, "Nice restaurant."

"Best chowder in Seattle five years running," she said with a practiced smile, obviously reciting the company line.

"How long have you worked here?"

"Eight or nine months."

"Would you happen to know if it's been redecorated in the last, say, two years?"

"This place?" She chuckled. "No," she said. "The management's view is if it ain't broke, don't fix it and we pack this place in the summer. Tourists like the ambience and locals like the food."

He smiled as she wandered off on her mission of keeping the five people in the restaurant content until tip time.

"Behind a picture?"

"Worked at your house with the computer disk, might work here," Katie said, dabbing her smiling lips with her napkin. She stood up and moved to examine several of the large, framed photographs, touching them as if to admire their totally pedestrian frames. "Bolted to the wall," she said, sitting.

"Behind the bar?"

"Too awkward."

"Taped to the bottom of a table?"

"I work in bars and restaurants. They clean those fairly often. How about heater vents?"

"Kind of dangerous, and besides, the ones here are located up toward the ceiling. What about looped in one of the fishnets hanging on the walls or stuck to a knickknack?"

She looked around this time, then shook her head. "It's cluttered in here, but it's not dirty. It's not even dusty. I bet they regularly clean every doodad."

Nick stood up and scanned the restaurant from this slightly elevated vantage point. He couldn't see a single place that something could be tucked away, no matter how small, that wouldn't have been discovered, either in routine housekeeping or in everyday use. It seemed hopeless.

"I'll go check out the men's room," he said with a sigh, and investigated a few little corners and moldings on his way.

The bathroom was small and clean and judging by the strip of a slightly different color showing under the paper hand-towel dispenser, newly painted. He frisked it anyway and then looked up. There was a fluorescent light fixture on the ceiling and for a moment he thought he'd found a good hiding place. The cover was clear plastic, however, and spotless. It appeared to be brand spanking new. There was also a vent on the ceiling, about a foot square. He dug out his pocketknife and flipped open the small screwdriver. Working quickly above his head, he easily removed the vent cover.

Knife back in his pocket, he felt around inside the opening. Nothing but metal walls. He couldn't reach any kind of bend in the pipe that would form a platform up inside the pipe, but one might exist right out of reach. His father was a smaller man than Nick, with a proportionately shorter reach. Might he have thrown something up inside there if he was desperate?

Nick opened the bathroom door, checked to see that there was no anxious-looking male approaching the restroom, then closed the door again. This time he climbed on top of the sink and stretched out toward the open vent and looked up inside.

He hadn't felt a shelf of any kind, because there wasn't one for three or four feet. If what they were looking for had landed way up there, Nick would need a flashlight and a stick with a brush of some kind on the end. And a guard outside the door.

He made it back to the floor but was still holding the cover when the door opened and a young restaurant employee entered.

"Damn thing fell right off the ceiling and just about hit me on the head," Nick said, depositing the four little screws and the vent cover in the startled kid's hands.

"I'm sorry, sir. I'll call the manager—"

"No problem," Nick said. "Don't worry about it."

He found Katie standing right outside the restroom door. She shoved his coat into his hands and grabbed his arm. "What took you so long? I sent the busboy in there to tell you to hurry."

"Don't you want to know if I found something?" he asked as she hustled him through the restaurant. "Hey, Katie, stop. Did you pay our bill?"

She tugged on him again. "Of course I paid the bill," she said as they erupted onto the sidewalk. "And I know you didn't find anything because I did."

"What!" He ground to a halt again, shrugging on his jacket and gloves. "Where—"

"Hurry," she pleaded, glancing beyond him. He turned to see what she was staring at. Through the haze, he found a huge passenger-and-vehicle ferry that had apparently docked at the pier next door while he'd been away from the table. A modest line of pre rush-hour cars were leaving the ship as fog-blurred pedestrian shapes moved along the elevated walkways connecting the ship's deck to the top floor of the terminal.

"What's going on?" he asked as he allowed Katie to pull him down the sidewalk.

"Look at the name," she said anxiously. "On the ferry, Nick. Look at the name."

He found the name high on the boat, scrolled into a board, painted black, just barely visible as the fog swirled around it.

Emerald Star.

Chapter Fourteen

Holding hands, Nick and Katie dashed across the street to retrieve the rental car. What followed was a hair-raising trip to the terminal parking lot only to find they needed to proceed a few blocks farther south, make a U-turn and return to enter in the proper lane. Nick did this as Katie held on for dear life and silently chanted, *hurry, hurry.*

They forked over cash to the ticket agent as Katie read from a sign. "It's the Bremerton Ferry," she said. "Says here it's a fifty-five-minute trip across Puget Sound."

"That's going south. Makes sense," Nick said.

As they were one of the last cars through the gate, they were waved immediately onto the boat, pulling to a stop behind a red truck that dwarfed their little rental compact. Another big vehicle, this one a gray SUV, pulled up behind them. Both drivers got out of their cars at once and headed for an internal stairway dividing the parking deck into three sections, a single lane on each side and a double lane in the middle. Ramps at either end of the ferry led to a second deck of parking.

Nick clicked off the engine and turned to Katie. "Let's try a new scenario. My father knew he was being followed when he drove into Seattle. He didn't stop and park and try to get lost at the public market or in a restaurant. Instead, he drove straight to the ferries."

"Maybe he lost his tail while driving through the city."

"As far as I know, he'd never been here before. Who knows what route he took? Anyway, he gets down here just in time to speed onto this ferry, leaving the other guy high and dry. That gives him fifty-five minutes to hide whatever it is he had to hide."

"Or maybe he bought a round-trip ticket and had almost two hours."

Nick opened the car door and got out. There were a couple of dozen cars in sight but not one human being. For all intents and purposes, the deck was little more than a floating parking lot. Lots of privacy for their search, only what exactly were they searching for?

He thought of what his father had said, the rambling words. What would a man afraid for his life take from someone connected to organized crime? An insurance policy, he'd said. So what constituted an insurance policy?

The answer was so obvious it amazed him.

He turned back to the car in time to see Katie getting out, wrapping her pale blue wool scarf around her head. He said, "Not a ledge, Katie. *Ledger.* He took financial records from the mob."

Her approach slowed as she came around the car, staring at him, obviously considering what he said. "Of course. But in what form? Another CD?"

"Probably. But we can't be sure. It could have been a book or it could be audio, like on a tape. We'll have to keep an open mind."

"Where do we start?"

"You've been doing pretty good. You choose. Do we divide and conquer? Do we start at the bottom or the top, aft or forward?"

She bit her lip. "We start at the top," she finally said. "Together. At the pointy end."

SEEING AS IT WAS a car ferry, Nick explained, there was no pointy end. The bow became whichever blunt end pointed in the direction the boat currently headed.

They climbed the interior stairs, exiting on a huge deck that consisted of a large heated passenger lounge bookended with covered and open decks for observation. Looking aft, the city of Seattle had already disappeared into the heavy fog.

It was cold out in the open, and by mutual agreement, they went inside the cabin. A few long benches sported sleeping figures stretched out to catch a little shut-eye during the ride, while a few other benches and tables held small groups of people visiting with one another or reading. The walls were covered with huge framed photographs of the city.

If there was a more utilitarian ship than a car ferry, Katie couldn't imagine what it was. The *Emerald Star*'s purpose was to ferry cars, bicyclists and pedestrians and it did so in a no-frills manner that left little in the way of nooks and crannies to hide anything.

They found all the furniture bolted to the walls and floors. All the pictures were also secured. No handy cubbyholes, very little in the way of adornments, nothing that didn't look as though it was hosed down quite often, handled every day—like the traffic cones, or painted off and on over the years.

"If he felt safe leaving it on this ferry for two years, it has to be attached to something permanent," Nick said.

They split up. Katie took the starboard side, Nick the port. Katie sat on every unoccupied bench, felt under every table, pulled and pushed on anything that looked remotely loose.

They met at the far end of the cabin and walked back outside into the chill, this time at what passed on this voyage as the bow of the ship. A stairway leading up to the bridge was barricaded by a tall wire fence and a locked gate. Without a key or some good wire cutters, they weren't going to get through now any more than Nick's father would have been able to get through two years before.

The metal bulwark handrails seemed to interest Nick, and Katie paused as he knelt down to investigate one.

"They're all shaped like an upside-down U with a flat bottom," he said. "Maybe he was able to jam something up inside one of them."

"There are miles of the things," Katie said.

They sat down on one of the outside benches. It was foggy and cold—they were the only people braving the open deck. But in the summer, the ferry would likely have been crowded and, depending on the time of the day, packed to the gills with commuters. Katie mentioned this to Nick and he sighed.

Katie had seldom in her life admitted defeat and she wasn't about to now, though she was close to admitting profound discouragement. Maybe she was wrong, maybe the ferry wasn't the answer to the riddle. Maybe whatever Nick's father had left as his life-insurance policy was already gone, washed away during a hose down or discovered by someone who had no idea what it was.

Nick said, "Let's use our heads."

"Mine is about ready to explode," Katie said.

He took her gloved hand in his, tucking her hair beneath the scarf and smiling. "We can't have that."

"Can't have what?"

"Your pretty head exploding."

She leaned forward and rested her forehead against his shoulder. His arm wrapped around her shoulders and, for a moment, she pretended they were two lovers sitting on a shipboard bench, striking out across the water, on a trip or sightseeing. Maybe Lily was there, too. Maybe she leaned against Katie's other arm, humming and happy.

"Okay, no exploding head," she said, pushing herself, and her fantasy, away.

"I was thinking about what you said about crowded decks and the cabin—and also my father's trip to Seattle," Nick said. "First he sees Patricia killed and decides to leave before he has to face me. He's so determined to avoid any emotional situation that he doesn't even go back to my house to collect his things including the CD outlining a hefty chunk of change. Instead he gets in his car and leaves Alaska. It must have taken him a couple of days of hard driving to get here. Then he realizes he has a tail."

"Okay, but answer this. He came all the way from Alaska. How did he pick up a tail?"

"Maybe a letter or phone call he made

from the road was intercepted. We'll probably never know for sure, but he said he had one, so let's go with that. If we're right and he drove onto this ferry, he might wonder if he was still being watched. He could be sure he was the last car, for instance, but he couldn't be sure he was the last person aboard."

"You mean his tail might have abandoned his car at the ferry parking lot and walked aboard as a passenger."

"Exactly. So there Dad is, cowering in his car. He's got his life-insurance policy and damn little else. The bad guy might be on board."

"What would you do?" Katie said.

He thought for a moment. "I'll tell you what I wouldn't do. I wouldn't come running up here and risk bumping into someone. I wouldn't stay in my car too long, either. Anyone could come looking for it—and me. I'd get out of my car, stash my evidence in a way that would attract no attention from anyone, and then I'd climb into an unlocked vehicle or camper. I'd leave my car on the ferry and take my chances driving off with some poor unsuspecting tourist."

"So that narrows our search to the two parking decks."

"Three sections on each deck. *If* I'm right." He glanced at his watch. "We have forty-three minutes before the boat docks. We can always turn around and ride it back to Seattle, but remember, he probably didn't do that, so think like he would have—hurried and desperate."

Katie got to her feet. "That shouldn't be hard," she said drily, thinking of the huge ticking clock hanging over her mother's head.

Unless they found what they were looking for and called the number Nick's father had given them. Unless they figured out how to get her back alive without using Nick's father as a bargaining tool.

Unless.

KATIE TOOK the starboard while Nick took the port. They started on the second-to-lowest deck. The ferry down here contained only a few permanently attached accoutrements on which to hide anything. The office was closed tight and that left the metal bulwarks and the inverted U-shaped rails that Nick had mentioned earlier. Katie took off her right glove to heighten her ability to feel what she touched. Even though she was technically indoors, there were dozens of windows and the fog outside pressed against the glass.

Eventually, Katie's search led her down the ramp to the bottom deck. Nick had reached this point before her and stood by an orange cone. The look on his face was enough to tell Katie he'd been no more successful than she had.

"My hand is frozen," she said.

"Mine, too. Let's take the outside lanes first."

Katie nodded and started along the starboard outside lane, once again running her numb fingers up inside the metal rail, feeling for anything unusual. She could scarcely believe it when her fingers bumped into something.

Bending over, she pried at the lump with frozen fingers, hoping it wasn't gum or something else disgusting. She couldn't bend low enough to look back up inside, but there was something there.

She tore off her left-hand glove and felt around with marginally warmer fingers.

A wad of tape. Edges thick, fraying, a

little gummy. Not much of it. Disappointment flooded her.

She continued searching until she was ten or fifteen feet away when she had second thoughts about abandoning the tape and walked back to where she'd found it.

This time she dug in her shoulder bag for something to use to pry at the tape. No nail file, but she did come up with her apartment key and used that.

Eventually, she was able to lift away a corner and thereby grasp the tape between her fingertips. Exerting a steady, gentle force, she felt it give way.

A little thrill ran up her spine as the tape fell into her hand. It weighed far too much to be tape alone. Holding it toward the closest window, she found embedded in the rectangular piece of gray duct tape a small metal object wrapped in plastic. Digging at this a little, she uncovered enough of what was inside the plastic to know she'd struck pay dirt.

What she held was a black-and-silver item with a sliding cover. It was about half the size of a pack of gum and she knew instantly what it was.

Nick's father had mumbled "thumbnail."

Her mind had leaped immediately to tales of ghastly torture before she pushed the word and the images it conjured as far from her mind as possible.

Not torture. This little thing. A flash drive, or thumbnail drive as it was sometimes called. Plugged into a computer, the operator could download just about anything into its memory. Things like crooked mob ledgers, for instance. The device could be locked, strung on a lanyard and carried around the neck or dropped in a pocket, toted off to a different computer, plugged in and called up, revealing everything stored in its memory.

Nick's father's life-insurance policy.

She had to find Nick. Closing the taped, crusted thumbnail drive in her hand, she took a step, then stopped abruptly.

A man had materialized from behind a nearby car. He pointed a gun at her. "I'll take that," he said, stretching out his free hand.

He was tall with oversize features and gaunt cheeks. Wiry black hair stood straight up in the damp weather. He wore a tan trench coat belted around his waist and held the gun, fitted with a silencer, as though he was used to holding it, as though it was an extension of his hand. His black eyes were as flat as snake eyes.

Katie barely registered these quick impressions before she turned and ran.

She heard a popping sound and the ping of metal behind her. She ran faster, toward the stern of the boat, away from death. Another popping sound.

"Nick!" she screamed as she ran onto the open stern of the boat. A length of heavy chain was secured across the back opening. Katie jumped over it, landing on her right leg which immediately gave way. She sprawled on the deck for just a moment, pain surpassed by fear as she scrabbled to her feet. It was either run back toward the gunman, leap into the water, or fling herself onto the slippery narrow deck that ran alongside the ferry sides.

Not one good option among them.

She stepped onto the deck, holding onto the tiny rail attached to the steep ferry side, her feet sliding. Flattening herself, she sidled along a few steps, her gaze drawn down to the opaque, churning water just six or seven feet below her. The wind whipped her scarf from her head and she watched as it flew off into the fog.

Who was this man? He had to be connected to Nick's father or the mob. Obviously, he wanted the thumbnail drive she still grasped in one hand. He had to have been aboard the ferry since they left Seattle; the attack had come after she found what they were looking for.

If push came to shove and she had to choose between saving Nick and holding on to the one thing that would save her mother, what would she do?

Where was Nick? Had the gunman shot him before he came looking for Katie? No, no, of course not. Nick couldn't be hurt. She wouldn't let him be hurt. Men like Nick didn't get hurt.

Sure they did...

The gunman finally caught up, skidding to a stop just shy of the chain, limping badly and breathing heavily. He stared toward the open back of the ferry. Did he expect to see her head bobbing in the wake? What could anyone see out there in that fog-covered water? She shrank against the side of the ferry and watched as he stepped over the chain, still holding the gun, though now the wind blew his trench coat open and it flapped around behind him, half hiding the firearm. All he had to do was turn around and he'd see her. She didn't dare move an inch.

She heard a sound coming from the deck above. Was Nick up there? Could he see the gunman standing out in the fog? Could he see the man was armed?

The engine noise plus the sound of the water at the stern must have obscured the sound Katie heard overhead; the gunman seemed oblivious to it. Once he turned around, however, he would face the ramp on which Nick—if it was him—would appear. And he would see her.

She crept back toward the stern, expecting at any moment for the man to hear her approach. But he kept staring into the water. Katie inched along, intent now on getting close enough to stop him…

The gun came up as Katie launched herself at his knees, knocking them both to the deck, the shot going wild as they both rolled close to the edge. He recovered first, catching her by her hair, yanking her toward him, the gun pointed at her throat. She flung her hand over the stern, opening her palm enough for him to see the taped mass that held the thumbnail drive. "I'll drop it," she said, gasping.

He yanked her hair again, grinning down into her face as the gun now dug into her back. "Go ahead," he said. "I've changed my mind about that thing. Who cares what Benito wants? I'll settle for you."

"Me?"

"You," he said, laughing softly.

"You tried to shoot me—"

"This is better," he said. "Now all I have to do is wait for Nick Pierce to show up. What do you think, sweetheart? Think he'll turn over his old man and a million dollars in exchange for you?"

"Nick isn't the kind of man to trade one hostage for another," Katie said brazenly.

"Even if it means losing his woman?"

"His woman? I'm not—"

"Shut up," he snapped, the gun jabbed fiercely into her spine. "You better hope you're his woman or you'll end up as dead as his wife."

His wife! What did this man know about Nick's wife? She had to know. She said, "Patricia died in an accident. She—"

He leaned close and whispered in her ear, his voice full of malice. "I wouldn't be too sure about that accident," he said. "Nick Pierce's wife was in the wrong place at the wrong time. An innocent bystander," he added, laughing deep in his throat. "Kind of like you."

Chapter Fifteen

With his back against the bulwark, Nick inched his way down the car ramp toward the stern of the boat. The fog was worse than ever but, through a window, he could see Katie standing ramrod straight in front of a man with bristly black hair.

He recognized him from the attack of the day before. Carson.

How had he gotten here?

Nick had already drawn his gun. He'd heard Katie scream his name and the sound of her running.

His mind whirled with unanswered questions, but none of that mattered. The boat would soon begin slowing down as it prepared to dock in Bremerton. People would show up. Katie was bait, he knew that, and probably expendable bait. As soon as Carson was reasonably sure Katie's survival was more of a liability than a benefit to him, he'd likely kill her and disappear.

Nick sneaked a little farther down the ramp and took aim. But the fog was too thick and Carson held Katie too close, shielding himself with her body. He'd even tucked his head close to hers, his free hand tangled in her hair. Nick couldn't take a chance he'd hit Katie.

Still holding the gun, he walked down the ramp like a man instead of a mouse. Easy to be brave when you had no choice.

His eyes met Katie's as she turned toward his advance. No smile this time, no light in her eyes, only terror.

Fire raged in Nick's gut. Carson would pay for doing this to her.

"Let her go," he called.

Katie cried out as Carson jerked on her hair, exposing her long throat. She appeared ready to faint, but the moment she managed to meet his gaze again, he saw a spark ignite her eyes. In the space of a heartbeat, he went from worrying she was about to collapse to worrying she might do something rash.

Carson smiled, shouted, "I've been in Seattle twenty-four hours waiting for you,

Pierce. Have to admit I was kind of hoping your dad might be along for the ride."

Nick stopped on his side of the chain. "He wasn't feeling up to the trip. How about you? Looks as though your thigh is bleeding where I shot you the last time."

Carson shrugged. "I ran on it, what can I say? Your little friend here is faster than she looks."

"So, what do you want from me?" Nick said.

"Your gun for starters," Carson said.

"Seems unlikely I'd just hand it over."

The muzzle of the silencer was suddenly pressed into Katie's throat. "Maybe not," Carson said.

Nick lowered his gun, clicked on the safety and threw it off the ferry.

Carson laughed. "Good."

"Now what? The money?" He slowly put his hand in his jacket pocket and took out the CD. "How about we trade? Me and the money for the woman. She has nothing to do with this."

"Too late for chivalry," Carson said, his eyes glued to the CD like a hungry man focused on a juicy steak. "But your cooperation will mean she'll suffer less in the end."

Katie opened her mouth to speak. Carson pulled her hair again. Her eyes watered as she cried out.

"Take it from him," he growled into her ear and loosened his grasp on her hair. She bent forward, hand extended.

As Nick handed her the disk, she winked at him. Before he could frown a warning for her to bide her time, she threw her head back, hitting Carson's nose, twisting her body at the same time. Her sudden struggle was so quickly and forcibly done and Carson's attention so riveted on the CD, that it actually worked. She was free of him. Nick kicked Carson's gun arm, the gun flew. Katie scrambled to retrieve it as Carson started to back up.

Blood streaming from his nose, Carson reached into his pocket. Nick saw the flash of another gun and knew this was it. He dove at Carson's knees at the same moment he heard a muffled shot. The tall man fell backward off the boat into Puget Sound, disappearing under the churning wake.

Nick jumped to his feet and turned to find Katie standing with Carson's gun in her hand. She was staring at the ferry wake. Nick scooped up the small gun Carson had been about to use to kill him and had apparently dropped before going overboard. He deposited it in his pocket, along with the CD he still grasped in his hand. Katie didn't say a word.

The sound of the boat engines changed. People would be showing up any moment. Fitted with a silencer, Carson's gun was unwieldy and heavy, yet Nick had to pry Katie's fingers from the grip. Throwing his arm around her trembling shoulders, he tossed that gun into the deep, gray water.

The two of them stared aft until a ferry employee finally showed up and demanded they get back on the right side of the chain, shaking his head at their foolishness.

Katie didn't seem to have the will or the strength to move. He gently lifted her in his arms, stepped over the chain and carried her toward their rental car.

"Nick?"

"It's okay," he told her, looking deep into her eyes, trying not to think about that moment when he'd thought for sure he'd never hold her again.

"I've never killed anyone before."

"It's okay," he repeated.

But he knew it wasn't.
Not yet.

CAROLINE CLOSED her eyes.

The flashlight was long dead. The apples were gone. She had no idea how long she'd been trapped in her increasingly horrible underground cell. The air wasn't too bad, thanks to the tiny ventilation pipe, but it was cold and dismal and scary and she'd had about as much as she could take.

Part of her doubted anyone would ever come. She shied away from thinking about her earthly remains lingering for decades until she was finally found and became the subject of one of those cold-case files on television.

She amused herself for a while picturing who they would get to play her. Some fading middle-aged actress, she decided, the one whose name she couldn't remember. Yeah. She'd be perfect. Jacqueline something, right? Or was it Rachael?

Never mind.

They'd include scenes from her past, of course. It was always interesting for the people sitting at home in easy chairs to speculate on how a person came to die in such a terrible, lonely way. Matt, her first husband, might tell them a thing or two—if they ever found him. Tess didn't know her father's name. Caroline had tended her secrets with care, keeping them close, keeping Tess safe. And Katie—well, she didn't know her mother was alive, not unless Matt had told her and they'd sworn they would never, ever say a word.

Caroline sighed deeply, then coughed. The cough had come on within the past few hours. It was deep and wet and it hurt her chest. Chills came with it, the kind that shuddered to the surface from deep within your body. She tried to get comfortable.

As soon as her eyes closed, she was back to the point in her past when monumental decisions had to be made, decisions everyone she cared about would have to live with forever. She wanted out of her marriage, but she didn't want to be alone. Matt refused to let go of his daughters. In the end, they'd made an agreement with the devil. The girls were very young, just six months old. They'd each take one and raise her as a single parent. They would never breathe a word about it to anyone.

Luckily, there was no one to ruin this plan.

She had abandoned her family the moment she married Matt and had had no contact with them since then. Matt had no living family. No grandparents, no aunts or uncles, not even a stray cousin. No one to spill the beans.

And so they separated, Matt producing a pair of dice, her rolling snake eyes, so numb to life by then that she didn't even grasp the irony of gambling, the very thing that had eaten away at their marriage being used to decide something as important as which adult took which baby. It just hadn't mattered. Matt had held on to Katie and she'd scooped up Tess, moving far away. Starting over.

And now, twenty-six years later, here she was, sitting in a hole, lost and dying.

Wasn't life odd?

Why did people cling to it when all hope was gone? But they did, because all hope wasn't gone until the last breath. Tears streaked her dirty cheeks.

She folded her knees against her chest and waited for the end.

AT NICK'S INSISTENCE, they bought a prepaid cell phone at a drugstore outside Bremerton.

"I don't want there to be any way to connect the call back to us," he told Katie when she pointed out she had a perfectly good cell phone in her suitcase, one that finally showed a signal. "Never forget this is organized crime we're talking about."

It took longer to drive back to Seattle than go by ferry, but Katie couldn't face another journey on the boat. She kept waiting for someone to nab her and accuse her of murder. Nick seemed to understand.

Murder. Never in her wildest dreams had she ever thought she would shoot a man dead. And yet she hadn't hesitated. She'd seen Carson reach into his pocket and that was it. She'd reacted as fast and as dispassionately as a lightning bolt. The creep was going to kill Nick, kill Lily's father. No way, not when she could stop it.

And now Carson was dead, spiraling to the bottom of the sound, and she was shaking inside. Quaking.

On their way back to Seattle, Nick pulled into an empty parking lot of a closed-down lumber mill and they both got out of the car.

"It's time we made the call," he said. "Okay with you if I do the honors?"

"Go ahead," she said as she leaned against

her side of the car, her back to him, staring ahead. The fog was getting to her, reducing the size of the world to a few feet in any direction, damp and cold and oppressive.

Nick came around to her side of the car, putting his hands on either side of her, leaning close. "Thank you," he whispered, looking into her eyes.

She knew why he was thanking her. Not for letting him make the call he was far more qualified to make than she was, but for his life. For doing something he knew she hated in order to save him. She flung herself against him and he folded his strong arms around her. He held her like that for several moments, rocking her, and she felt comforted in a way she hadn't for a long time. He'd been gentle on the ferry, carrying her when she couldn't walk, talking to her in a soothing voice she could barely hear over the roar in her head. She'd been numb with shock.

But she wasn't numb anymore. Quite the contrary. She was acutely aware of every inch of his hard, lean body as it pressed against hers. Of his hands gripping her back. Of his warm breath caressing her neck, of his broad chest upon which she rested her head.

He couldn't be comforting to her, not really, not for long. He wasn't her father. He was a man she wanted to want her. Having his kindness was nice, but it wasn't enough. It would never be enough.

And she knew if she looked up at him all teary-eyed, he'd kiss her. How she longed to do just that. But a kiss wasn't enough, either. And he'd made it clear a kiss was all he would offer.

And factored into this was the memory of what Carson had said about Nick's wife's death. Was it really not an accident? Had the car been aimed at Nick's father? It could explain why Bill had left the "accident" scene so abruptly. If Bill had seen Carson behind the wheel and realized his presence in Nick's life had just resulted in Patricia's injury, Bill might have reacted with a sort of valor: get out of town before Nick and Lily were the next to be hurt.

Or maybe Carson had said all that to terrorize Katie. It had worked. She'd frozen. Maybe it wasn't true.

She couldn't bring this up with Nick right that moment, not out here in a foggy parking lot. He'd need time to consider this and think and mourn again. She couldn't ask him to toss off this startling news without privacy. They had a job to do.

She disentangled herself from his embrace. "Let's get this over with," she said.

He nodded, but his attention stayed on her face longer than necessary, and she fancied she could feel heat rising up her neck. It was as though he knew exactly what she was thinking. All of it. The evasions, the longing…everything.

From his wallet, he extracted the scrap of paper he'd taken from his father's pocket just a day or so before. He turned on the phone and punched in the numbers, then looked at Katie as he hit Send.

Katie paced up and down the weed-infested asphalt, staring at Nick as he waited for someone to answer the phone. She stopped breathing when he finally said, "Yes. It's Bill Thurman. I have what you want. How's my wife?"

Nick had pitched his voice deeper and somehow sounded as though he had a head cold. He was portraying himself as his father…

He listened for a second before saying, "With all due respect, Benito, I don't trust you any more than you trust me. You're not getting anything until I see my wife, until I take her hand. I'll hand over the ledger then and there, but not the money. Sure, I still have your money, what did you think, I'd spend it? The money is my way out of this. You'll get it when I get my wife back and not a second before."

What were the chances Benito would agree to that? Katie opened her mouth to protest and closed it without speaking. She'd given the job of contacting this man to Nick. When had she seen him ever do anything he hadn't thought out?

Nick said, "I can find it. Sure. Okay. Bring a computer." He listened for another minute or two and said, "I understand. Midnight. Before any of this happens, though, I need to know she's okay. Let me talk to her." More waiting, and then he hung up the phone.

"Did they let you talk to her?" Katie demanded.

"No. They said she's not with them." He took a pencil out of his pocket and scribbled a list of directions on the paper with the phone number. "We have eight hours to get back to Seattle and arrange things," he said, approaching her.

"Arrange what?"

"I'll tell you in the car. It's time we got some help. There's just one thing I want you to keep in mind. This is organized crime we're talking about. If Benito or any of his buddies ever find out who we are, we're dead meat."

"That's why you used your father's name."

"Exactly. They already know about him. Carson is dead, so we're safe there. If we can pull this off, my father and your mother can disappear into a witness-protection program."

Katie said, "Disappear—"

"They'll have to, honey."

Tears burned behind Katie's nose. Was he telling her that her mother was going to be whisked away the moment they found her? What about Tess? Tess needed to see her mother. Needed to hold her and be comforted and introduce her fiancé, Ryan Hill, and make wedding plans… What about Tess?

What about me? Katie admitted to herself. *After all this, am I never going to have the chance for a heart-to-heart talk? I need to understand how she could leave me. Will I be denied that in the rush?*

"There's no other way," Nick said. "It's not just Benito—you know, it's the organization that stands behind him as well. From the way he talked just now, Benito didn't seem to know Carson had followed your father to Alaska, maybe even that he took him there himself to retrieve the money. Benito seemed surprised my father still had the money. Maybe Carson was supposed to trail my dad and keep an eye on him, but maybe in the end he got excited about recovering the money for himself, never planning on telling Benito anything about it. At any rate, we can't be sure Benito isn't expecting Carson to contact him. When he doesn't, they may come looking for him and that might lead him to us. I don't want to disappear forever, do you?"

She blinked back the tears, figuratively squared her shoulders and abandoned self-pity. "No, I don't want to disappear forever." *Unless it's with you and Lily* was her next, unspoken thought, but it wasn't true. She liked her life. She had plans! She had no desire to become someone else. She'd done that for a few weeks after her father died, before a hit-and-run driver put her in the hospital. It had been lonely and scary and she didn't want to do it again.

"I'm going to make sure we have a life-insurance policy," Nick added.

"Just like your dad," she said.

He stared at her.

"I'm sorry. I shouldn't have made a comparison. Listen, Nick. There's something I need to tell you—"

"Can it wait?" he whispered, his face so close she could almost taste him.

She stared at his well-formed lips. "Yes," she finally said. "It can wait."

But she couldn't.

She'd take what she could get. She closed the gap between them, touching his lips with hers, a surge of pure molten lava pulsing through her body, heating her mouth, her touch, crying out to him silently, praying he could hear her.

Praying he wanted to.

Chapter Sixteen

Caroline heard the noise in her sleep.

She'd been dreaming of the day she left Matt. Of Katie sitting up in her crib, innocently watching her mother and sister getting ready for a trip.

Of the last kiss and the tears that had slipped from Caroline's eyes and fallen on Katie's round, pink cheeks.

Her car was in the driveway. Matt was warming up the engine. It was old, he said. You had to warm it up before you drove it. Pretty soon she'd be gone and she wouldn't warm it up if she didn't want to.

He'd taken Tess from her for a moment, kissed her forehead, handed her back, watched as Caroline buckled the baby in her car seat.

Katie inside the house, behind the door. Tess in a car seat, bound for…

Caroline didn't know where. She didn't care.

She and Matt had looked at each other then. Maybe for the first time in weeks, they'd studied each other's faces, looking perhaps for a sign of weakness, waiting for one of them to cry foul and call it all off, put their family back together again, ready to limp along into the future.

Neither of them blinked. Caroline had put the car in gear and driven away.

The car sounded funny. There was something wrong with the engine. She wouldn't be able to leave if the old wreck broke down now, and her heart started hammering.

She cried out and woke suddenly.

The engine noise came from outside, the first noise she'd heard in days.

Her heart pounded painfully against her ribs, rattling in her shell of a body. She coughed into her hand and shivered.

She heard voices. Someone was coming.

More noise and she shielded her eyes as her roof suddenly disappeared. Three men stood above her, their faces obscured by the bright lights they shone in her eyes. She threw up an arm to protect her vision. She saw guns. One man said something and the others laughed and she knew it was because it looked as though she'd turned into a wild animal in that hole.

She didn't bow her head. When they yelled at her to stand up, she stood, without help, wavering on her feet, faint headed, the cough rattling her chest. But she stood and breathed in the fresh, cold, wet air.

And scanning the men until she could finally see a face.

Her voice hoarse, she demanded, "Where in the hell is Bill? What have you done with my husband?"

THE DRIVING INSTRUCTIONS Nick was given over the phone led to an abandoned construction site out in the middle of nowhere. He drove along a dirt road, lights jouncing and car lurching as it dipped into potholes and rattled across abandoned odds and ends.

The road didn't look as though it had been traveled in years, but of course there could be half a dozen ways in and out. It was too dark to tell if anyone else was already there.

He had a bad feeling about this. It didn't take a Rhodes Scholar to figure out Benito wasn't going to let anyone walk who might be able to finger him. Frankly, he was doubtful that Caroline was still alive, though he hadn't shared that insight with Katie. The fact that Benito hadn't allowed her to talk to him was worrisome, as was the fact that his father had seen and talked with Benito and his associates. If Caroline had seen their faces, too, she was dead.

He'd kept the money out of the exchange in the feeble hope that getting that back would delay any retaliation against him. It was his one slim chance.

There could very well be a shallow grave already dug out in this mess. There could be another one, wide open and waiting—for him. His headlights picked out deep depressions in the distance, foundation footings no doubt. Stacks of rusting rebar, scattered lumber and piles of bricks also sculpted the landscape. What little breeze there was ruffled battered lengths of ghostly plastic sheeting. At least it wasn't foggy this far inland.

The last several hours had seen a flurry of activity. The drive to Seattle, a meeting, phone calls, talking, shopping. They were here now, though Nick would have given a great deal to be alone, to know that Katie was safe somewhere behind him. She'd argued that since no one was expecting her, she'd be perfect to cover his back. This was crazy, of course, but he wasn't her keeper. He had no right to tell her how much or how little she should be involved in rescuing her mother.

Hell, she hadn't seen the woman since she was a few months old. He sensed there was more going on here for Katie than a rescue attempt.

They only had one gun, the one Carson had dropped as he fell overboard. Katie had a license to carry, thanks to her late father's urging, and she knew how to protect herself, but she refused to even hold it. He knew she was still hurting over killing Carson, but he hated leaving her unarmed. The gun was in his jacket pocket. It would be his job to make sure no one got past him to harm her. Period. And to him that meant he'd sacrifice her mother if he had to. Katie would never forgive him if it came to that, but he'd just have to go through the rest of his life knowing she was alive to hate him.

"Stay down," he warned her. She'd consented to keep her head low, her profile invisible. So everything was as ready as it could get considering how foolhardy it suddenly seemed.

Beside him, Katie, reading his mind again, mused, "Funny how sensible this all seemed a couple of hours ago, isn't it?"

"Yeah," he said, glancing at her delicate face. "Get lower," he demanded. "All the way on the floor. Please."

She slid her seat way back and curled herself up on the passenger-side floor as he'd asked. It was a tight fit, even for someone as petite as she. And for some reason, staring down at her, his mind flashed to Lily.

But he couldn't think of Lily. He'd done what he could to protect her and provide for her and he would do everything in his power to return to her. But thinking about her tore his heart out of his chest, so he carefully put thoughts of her away in a private place. Katie was in there, too. At least she would be when this was over and she'd moved on with her life.

"The last two days have been so focused on finding the information your father hid," she mused. "Now that we have the ledger and the money, I have a terrible feeling it won't do us much good."

"Battleground jitters," he said, trying to make out her features in the dim light. He smiled broadly to boost her morale and added, "Remember. Don't let them see your face. Put on that mask we bought and keep it on. Your future depends on them not knowing who you are. No matter what happens, stay incognito."

"I got you," she said, slipping on the Snow White mask they'd purchased earlier that day. He leaned down to straighten it for her and she reached up and dabbed at the dark greasepaint she'd helped smear on his jaw, hoping to give the impression of an unshaved, older, at-the-end-of-his-rope husband.

He caught her hand and kissed her fingers. When he glanced out the windshield again, he saw a flashing light a few hundred yards away.

"There's my cue. Please, Katie, stay in the car," he said softly. "If you hear any shooting, for God's sake stay hidden till the smoke clears."

"I will."

He didn't believe her for a moment. She'd come running and get herself caught in the crossfire. "I mean it," he said seriously.

"Just go."

He got out of the car. No interior light went on because he'd taken the precaution of removing the bulb. He tugged on the cowboy hat he'd bought that afternoon and pulled it low, covering his hair and the upper part of his face. He zipped the coat that looked like the one his father had been wearing. When he walked, he tried to affect an anxious, shuffling manner, like a man twenty-five years older, a man worried sick about his wife. A stumble here and there, a swearword when he hit a rock. He pitched his voice lower to match the voice he'd used earlier that day on the phone and added the nasal quality.

"Stop shining that damn light in my face!" he yelled when he was almost there. He had one arm up and he slouched a little. Another fear was that if Caroline was still alive she'd realize Nick wasn't her husband and say something that would give him away.

The light lowered. He could see three men standing by a car. A smaller figure seemed to be tied up on the ground behind them, bent over in a sitting position, head bowed and resting on bent knees. His heart raced. That had to be Caroline and he'd just seen her head turn when he spoke.

"Where are my books?" one of the men called.

"That you, Benito?"

"Yeah, it's me, you dirty thief. I have half a mind to blow your brains out right this moment. You *and* the little woman."

Nick's grip on the automatic in his pocket tightened. "Come on now, Benito, no hard feelings, huh? I got your ledger right here."

"How about my money, you slimeball?"

Nick imitated a nervous chuckle. "I ain't that stupid. I don't have your money on me. You want your money, you give me my wife."

"Hand over the books, you crook," Benito said.

Nick said, "Catch," and threw the flash drive at the group of men. It pinged when it hit something on the ground. One man swept his flashlight until he found it. He seemed to be the brains of the outfit, as it was he who picked up the drive and took it to a laptop set up on the hood of the car, inserted it and clicked a few keys.

"It's not here, boss," he said. "It's all gobbledygook."

"It's a code, you moron. How about the pictures of me and Ciddici?"

"Yeah, they're here."

"Now I want my wife," Nick said.

"You come and get her."

"No, no. You send her to me."

"She's a little weak in the knees."

Nick's stomach turned over. He didn't try to keep his voice from reflecting his revulsion as he said, "Listen, you scumbag. If you hurt her—"

"What are you gonna do?" Benito called. "Come after me?"

"Just send her over here with one of your boys. He can walk us back to the car. I'll tell him where to find the money. We go our way, you go yours."

"*Now* you trust me?" Benito said.

"No way. Have your guy strip down to his skivvies. I'll keep him covered, you keep me covered."

"Mutual respect, I like that," Benito crowed with a belly laugh. He added, "Kenny. You been working out, you strip."

"It's cold out here. I don't—"

"Now." There was more bellyaching, but eventually Kenny stripped down to shoes, socks, boxer shorts and a T-shirt. Even in the indirect light, the man looked like a gigantic muscle.

With one hand, he grabbed Caroline's arm and pulled her to her feet. She cried out.

"Hey! Watch it!" Nick called. "Shine a light on her."

Kenny did. Dressed in flimsy pajamas, streaked with mud, she looked filthy, cold, frightened and sick. They'd gagged her. Nick could tell from her expression she had no idea who he was. If they'd left that gag out of her mouth, she would have given him away.

But she also looked as though she was in one piece, and there was little more he could do for her at the moment than get her out of there.

"Come on, Carrie," he said fondly. "We'll get you home."

Kenny started walking toward Nick, supporting Caroline's weight. Nick thought things would probably go okay until they got close to the rental car and then the fun would begin. The thing about a thumbnail drive no one had mentioned was the ease with which it could be copied. Nick hadn't mentioned it just to see if Benito would. Benito hadn't. There was no way Benito would ever let Nick and Caroline walk away that night when a dozen copies could be floating around in a dozen computers, even if it was doubtful anyone could read the code.

There would be gunfire; there would be a

battle. He'd arranged it; he expected it. Nick's main goal was to keep Katie and her mother safe.

He leaned down to Caroline and whispered, "Can you run?"

She shook her head. The whites of her eyes were huge in the reflected light, communicating quite clearly, *I can barely walk and you want me to run?*

"I'm going to carry her," he shouted, turning to look over his shoulder. "You swine mistreated her. She's too weak to walk!"

"Yeah, that's a good idea, you do that," Benito shouted back.

Nick picked her up effortlessly. This was where he had to make a leap of faith and trust other people to do what they'd promised they would do. The meeting earlier that day with the FBI had been awkward, though, full of half-truths and dangling sentences as Nick tried to keep Katie's involvement out of it. Had he succeeded? Had they staked out this place hours before Benito and his boys arrived? The head agent had said they would, and Nick had no choice now but to believe she had. Taking a deep breath, clutching Caroline close, he broke into a run.

He heard shouts as gunfire erupted behind him.

Sure enough, Katie had responded to the shots by running to meet him, reacting as she always did, leading with her heart. He put her mother down and turned to find Kenny in the middle of a flying dive. Nick launched himself in a counterattack, hitting Kenny in the stomach. The big man fell with a thud and Nick hit him over the head with his gun for good measure. Twice.

He didn't want to get caught with a gun last registered to a dead cop, so he stuck it back in his pocket and, crouching low with Katie and her mother, waited for the air to clear.

There were several new sources of lights as the gunfire petered out. The FBI had done their job. Benito was in handcuffs, one man was down, the computer was in custody. Nick helped Katie get her mother to her feet. "I'll be right back," he told Katie. "Stay covered."

She nodded, the smiling plastic mask covering everything but the glittering of her eyes.

Nick approached the agent he'd met with when he and Katie first arrived back in

Seattle after that fateful ferry ride. He'd known their only chance was to involve the law. "There's another one on the ground a few yards back there. He should be coming to any moment."

Agent Loni Boone smiled as she directed the medics to Kenny's position. "Is the woman okay?"

"She's okay."

"Good. I know we have the ledger, but like I told you when we met, it won't mean much without your father's testimony. I did hear Benito mention there was a picture of himself with Ciddici on that drive. That needs context. We need your father to come forward."

"He will."

"You said he was injured?"

"Yes, but expected to recover. I'll call his doctor later and check up on him."

"Tell me where he is and we'll go get him."

He smiled coldly, trying to imagine Doc's reaction to a plane full of FBI agents landing in his field. He said, "No. My father will come to you."

"I want Benito for more than kidnapping. I want him for extortion and racketeering."

"I know."

How was Nick going to explain his father's gunshot wound? Without Carson to blame it on, what could he say? He'd have to come up with a story—

"Benito and Ciddici have some very creepy associates," Agent Boone said firmly. "This project, for instance," she said, with a sweeping motion taking in the abandoned construction site, "is mob controlled, closed down in a legal battle with the former owners. One of them has disappeared and the other one is suddenly very quiet. Your father doesn't stand a chance on his own."

"I'll tell him."

"Well, Mr. Pierce, when you came in today and told me about all this, I thought you were nuts. I guess you weren't."

"Not so as you could tell," he said. "Okay with you if we take my stepmother to the hospital? She's in pretty rough shape and, well, she and her daughter need a little time to…reconnect."

"That's fine. We'll question all of you tomorrow, especially her, though from the look of that hole they had her in, I doubt she saw anything."

"Lucky for her," Nick said, shaking Boone's hand.

He walked away, stopping only when Boone called out. "We'll try and keep both your names out of this," she said.

"Much obliged," Nick said, tipping his cowboy hat. He kind of liked the thing.

As he approached the car, he slowed down. He could see two dark shapes in the back seat but heard no voices coming from the open door. Maybe he should give Katie and her mother a little time alone. He turned to look at the now-well-lit crime scene. Couldn't go back there. Police cars and ambulances had shown up and the area was a zoo. Professionals were busy gathering information and flashing pictures.

And Katie? It struck him suddenly that she now had what she wanted, what she needed: a family. She would be leaving now. He knew how anxious she was to grab every possible moment with her mother before her mother was whisked away into obscurity.

And her sister. She'd barely had a chance to introduce herself before they had to separate.

Katie was safe, Caroline was free.

Well, so was he.

KATIE TOOK OFF her coat and draped it over her mother's shoulders. It wasn't until Nick reached in and screwed back in the car light that she finally got a good look at her mother.

Her face was streaked with dirt. Her clothes were damp and moldy smelling, her breathing labored, her washed-out blond hair dirty and matted. A rattling cough suggested a bronchial infection. She sat very still beside Katie, looking down at her filthy hands until she suddenly began shaking, looking from Katie to Nick, who sat in the front seat staring back at her. Finally, she said, "Who are you people? What do you want with me? Where's Bill? Where's my daughter?"

Her questions came rapid fire, her gravelly voice threaded with fear.

Nick said, "Calm down. Everything is okay. You're safe. Bill is in good hands." Addressing Katie, he added, "Honey, you're still wearing your mask. It's safe now, you can take it off."

"Of course." Katie whipped off the mask.

Caroline's eyes flew wide-open. She said, "Tess?" but then she shook her head and said, "You're not Tess."

"No."

Tears filled Caroline's eyes. "Katie? Is it you? Am I still dreaming?"

"You're not dreaming," Katie said softly. She'd been waiting for this instant since the first moment she read her father's letter, given to her after his death, the first time she'd learned her mother hadn't really died during childbirth. And in the heartbeat it took her mother to assimilate the startling news, it dawned on Katie that she might be too late, that her mother might have preferred having only a single child to love and didn't need or want a duplicate daughter.

In the next heartbeat, Caroline threw her arms around Katie's neck and pulled her to her chest, pressing her so close it was hard for Katie to breathe. Then she pushed her away and searched her face, fingered her red hair, looking, it seemed, for some sign of the child she'd abandoned, looking for ways Katie resembled Tess, looking for who knows what. Over and over again, she whispered, "I'm sorry, I'm so sorry, I was wrong, Katie, forgive me."

Katie was only vaguely aware of Nick driving the car away from the construction site. She, too, was crying. There were still so many questions to be answered.

Katie dug her cell phone out of her pocket. She'd put it there hours before in the hope she would soon use it to call Tess with good news. She punched in the hospital number and Tess picked up almost immediately.

"Guess who I'm sitting next to?" Katie said.

Tess screamed. "Our mother?"

"Yes." Looking at Caroline, who still gripped Katie's free hand, she said, "Yes. *Our* mother."

Chapter Seventeen

It took some doing to find a shortwave radio with which to contact Doc, but someone at the hospital knew someone else with a brother-in-law who had a rig and, eventually, Nick drove to a stranger's house in the middle of the night to call his old friend.

"He's doing okay," Doc said. He sounded as though Nick had woken him up. "You got the bullet out, but it looks like you did the operation with your feet."

"Don't you remember, Doc? My job in the war was to get shot at. Your job was to patch me up."

"Yeah, I remember. Okay, what about his heart?"

"You were right. His wife says he has a mitral valve problem. He's scheduled for surgery in a few weeks." Nick read off a list of medications his father was supposed to take.

"Common stuff, I have it on hand," Doc said.

"When can he travel?"

"Not for at least a week. Maybe more. I need to go to Seattle to see wife number three, what's her name, Elaine. I'll fly down with him. You send money."

Nick smiled. "I'll cover your trip, too, Doc. Least I can do. The FBI is anxious to see him. I've stalled on his whereabouts, but you'd better get him here as soon as it's safe."

Nick said the last "over and out." His next call was from the car, using the disposable cell phone he'd bought to call Benito. He woke Helen up, as well.

"I suppose she's asleep," he said, with a sudden sweeping desire to hear his daughter's voice.

"Of course she's asleep. And you? You're okay?"

"I'm fine," he told her.

"What about that man?"

"You mean my father?"

"Yes. Is he out of our life for good?"

"Do you mean did he die? No, looks like he'll make it. I stashed him at Doc's place. I'll be on my way home soon. I got myself a motel room so I can catch some shut-eye." Reading off his receipt, he gave her the number of his room. "My plan is to catch a plane up to Juneau in the morning. I left the DeHavilland there. I'll call you from the airport."

"Sounds fine," Helen said. "There's another storm predicted—"

"There's always another storm predicted." It didn't matter to him. A storm wasn't going to keep him from Lily.

By the time he drove across town to the hospital, the sun was rising, and the fog had cleared. Seemed like an omen. Good weather for flying.

He found Katie asleep in a chair next to her mother's bed. Caroline's eyes were wide-open and she smiled anxiously when she saw Nick.

"Did you talk to Bill?" she whispered.

"I talked to his doctor. Told him about the heart situation. Everything is under control."

She nodded.

"Can't you sleep?"

"No. I can't bear to close my eyes. I can't bear the thought of dreaming."

He sat down in the free chair on the opposite side of the bed from Katie. "Dreaming?"

"More than dreaming," she said, pausing to cough into a tissue. "More like remembering. There's just too much I want to forget."

"It doesn't work that way," Nick said.

"I know it doesn't. But I've done some terrible things, Nick. It's okay if I call you that, right? Katie has filled my head with stories about you."

"Sorry about that," he said, glancing over at Katie. She looked so young and so peaceful.

"I can never tell you how much I appreciate what you've done for me and your father. Maybe now we can all be a family—"

"That can't happen," he said quickly, interrupting her fairy tale. "I'm not my father's son, Caroline. It's too late for all that. Didn't Katie tell you the Justice Department is willing to offer you and my father new identities in trade for his testifying at Benito's trial? It's his only chance for long-term survival. You'll have to make the choice of going with him or staying here with your girls."

She looked stricken. Her attention wandered over to Katie and she sighed. "How can I leave her again?"

He wanted to ask her how she could have

left her in the first place, left her with a man addicted to gambling, left her with no mother. But the pain in Caroline's eyes was so acute he didn't dare, and besides, Katie said she'd had a pretty good childhood, despite her father's problems. Maybe it had worked out the best it could.

He said, "It will take time for you to get better and for my father to mend. Time to arrange a trial. You'll have time, I think, for figuring out what's best to do, what you need to do, and time for getting reacquainted with Katie."

"And you?"

"I'm flying home tomorrow morning. I have a little girl who needs me."

"Lily," Caroline said.

"Yes."

"Katie couldn't stop talking about her, either."

Nick's throat closed. He tried clearing it and was horrified to find his eyes burning. Well, he hadn't slept in a long time. "When she wakes up, tell her I got a room in the motel across the street and that I'll look in one last time before I take the car back to the rental place and fly home," he said. "I need to get some sleep and you two have a lot of catching up to do."

Caroline looked slightly panicky. "What do I tell her?" she pleaded. "How do I explain myself?"

He stood up. "I don't know," he said. "I guess you try to make her see how it looked through your eyes all those years ago. Don't worry. Katie has the biggest heart in the world. She'll meet you halfway."

KATIE COULDN'T remember ever crying this much. Not even after her father died, not even when she awoke in the hospital to discover her twin sister injured. Never.

It was just all so sad. Her mother's brutal honesty left Katie gasping for breath, her heart aching. For herself. For Tess. For her father. And for her mother, most of all.

The woman had made some awful decisions, but so had her father, and his hormones hadn't been acting up, his body hadn't been tortured by postpartum depression. He'd also been older. He should have known better. It was amazing to Katie how arbitrary her parents had been to deny Tess and her their birthrights as twins—to grow up together, to be there for one another.

But it was over and there was nothing to

be served by withholding understanding and forgiveness.

On the heels of this emotional maelstrom, the FBI and the police showed up. She held her mother's hand during their interrogation. They informed her they'd already spoken with Nick, that they'd caught him as he left the hospital. Katie gave her own version of the hostage exchange, claiming truthfully that she'd been too far away to hear or see much. She knew there would be more questions to come.

It didn't matter. Nick had said to tell the truth with the exception of talking about Carson. Pretend he didn't exist in all this, Nick told her. If her name was ever connected to his death, the mob would come after her. As she had no desire to relive Carson's death, and her role in it, she found this incredibly easy to do.

But wouldn't his body eventually float to the surface, complete with bullet wounds? Wouldn't his identity be linked to Benito? Had anyone on the ferry seen what happened; would they come forward someday? The gun's silencer and the noise of the engines had muffled the gunshot, had the fog adequately obscured the view? Did Katie have to live the rest of her life with this hanging over her head?

After everyone had left, Katie and her

mother called Tess again and discovered she was in the process of checking herself out of the hospital. She and Ryan were driving up to Seattle the next day.

Time for a big reunion.

"Too bad Bill's son is leaving tomorrow morning," her mother said once they were off the phone. "He told me to tell you he'd stop by the hospital one more time to say goodbye. He's got himself a room across the street to catch up on his sleep."

Katie produced a wooden smile.

Of course Nick was leaving. What would possibly keep him here?

She swallowed back a burst of regret. Nick was leaving.

NICK WOKE UP the moment the motel room door opened. He sat up abruptly, blinking at the infusion of outside light that backlit his guest.

Katie. He'd have known her size and shape anywhere.

"How'd you get in here?" he asked, glancing at the clock. It was almost evening. He'd been asleep for seven hours.

"I told the motel clerk I was your wife and she let me in."

He rubbed his head with one hand. "Some security."

"You're leaving tomorrow," she said, as she closed the door and threw the room back into twilight.

He switched on the bedside lamp. "I would have come by to say so long."

She took off her coat. "Mind if I use your shower?"

"Of course not."

She disappeared into the bathroom with her suitcase while he lay back down and tried to close his eyes again, but of course, that was impossible with her so close by. Naked and wet. Standing in his shower.

She took her time in there. At last the water stopped running and then he waited.

He was sitting up in bed when she opened the bathroom door. She was holding a white towel around her body. Damp tendrils of red hair curved around her cheeks, curved around her throat.

He said, "Katie—"

But she stopped him with one finger held in front of her lips. "Don't," she said softly.

"Don't what? I was just going—"

"To tell me you're too old or too burned-out or too something or the other. To tell me

I'm too precious to waste on a man with no room in his heart. Something like that, right?"

She'd been advancing as she spoke. He ran a hand through his hair as he looked at her glistening skin, her full lips, her long, bare legs.

She let go of the towel. It fell to her feet in slow motion and she stood before him stark naked, more beautiful than any woman he'd ever seen, despite the lingering bruises.

More beautiful than Patricia?

Patricia. She was gone and suddenly it struck him how disappointed she'd be in what he'd become. Why had he forgotten how full of life she'd always been?

Katie was beautiful, just as Patricia had been, both in their unique way. And like Patricia, Katie set him afire.

"Katie," he said again.

"You don't want me," she said.

"I don't want you? Are you crazy?"

"I mean forever," she said. "It's okay."

"You don't—"

She stepped over the towel. In her hand, she held a foil packet that she set next to the lamp. Then she turned the lamp off. "Move over," she whispered into the dark. Once she'd slipped between the sheets and fit herself against him, filling his arms, breathing against his neck, she added, "If all we have is one night, let's make it count. Let's make it perfect."

And running his ravenous hands over her soft, exquisite body, he buried himself in her warmth.

THE RINGING PHONE woke them both a few hours later. Nick kissed Katie before answering it.

"Mr. Nick?" his housekeeper said. It was a lousy connection and he assumed she'd called to tell him the storm that was predicted was a fact. It passed through his mind that he might need to delay returning for a day or so. Glancing at Katie's upturned face, he smiled at the thought.

"What's up?" he asked.

"Come home," she said. "You…later—"

The first stirrings of alarm made Nick swing his feet to the floor.

"Helen? I can't make out what you're saying."

"—didn't know—just—"

It wasn't just the phone line—it was Helen. She sounded upset. Almost incoherent. Afraid. Nick's mind flew immediately to Lily.

"What's wrong?" he barked in such a way that Katie sat up. "Helen? Is it Lily?"

But the line was dead.

Heart thumping in his chest, he sat staring at the receiver, too startled to think.

"What is it?" Katie asked.

"The line is dead. She sounded frantic."

"Call her back!" Katie insisted.

Of course, why hadn't he thought of that? He called her number and got a busy signal. He hung up and waited a few moments, then tried again. Still busy.

Meanwhile, Katie scurried around the room, pulling on jeans and sweater, lacing shoes. "Nick? What is it? What did she say?"

"Practically nothing," he said, pulling on his own clothes. "Something about coming home. It was the way she sounded."

Once dressed, he called Helen again with the same results. He called information next, and got the number for the Vixen Hill police department. They answered on the first ring.

"I know the place," the officer on call said. "I know Helen, too. Saw her just yesterday in town with a little girl. Your kid, huh? Cutie. Listen, sir, I wouldn't be too alarmed. We've got wind and ice here and sometimes the lines go down for days. I'll get out to her cousin's place later this afternoon if the weather lets up. Call me back. And don't worry, I'm sure everything is fine."

Nick hung up the phone and stared at Katie.

"He told me not to worry."

"It's not his baby," Katie said. "What are you going to do?"

"Catch the next plane out of here," he said, throwing his clothes in his duffel. He had a gut feeling. Life had taught him not to ignore a gut feeling.

Maybe he hadn't been so clever, after all. Maybe Benito had known all along where Bill Thurman would go to retrieve his money. Maybe he sent Carson along to watch over things. And maybe he sent someone else along to watch over Carson. When Bill and Carson more or less disappeared, maybe this wild card stayed in Alaska, waiting for word the deal was done.

But the word didn't come. Instead Carson was missing and Benito was in jail.

Maybe Benito knew that short of killing him, the one surefire way to stop Bill from testifying against him was to threaten Lily Pierce, Bill's one and only granddaughter.

If so, he hadn't figured on Nick.

Chapter Eighteen

Katie packed her own suitcase in a hurry. Nick was going to drive to the airport and fly to Juneau on the next available flight. He told her to keep the motel room, that she and her sister would need someplace to stay, but she couldn't sit there by herself.

She'd go to her mother's room and await Tess. She'd take care of her family while Nick took care of his.

So, why did it feel so wrong?

It wasn't until Nick pulled into the hospital parking lot that she knew why it felt wrong: because it *was* wrong.

Tess and her mother were family, yes, but they weren't the family that had taken root in her heart, not yet. Nick and Lily were that family, even if she wasn't that family for them. She didn't know if that made sense, but it was the way it was.

She'd given herself to Nick with no strings. But that didn't mean strings didn't exist. She'd known the moment she slipped into his bed that she was in love with him and that would have to be enough for both of them.

Maybe Nick was wrong and the phone lines had simply gone down with the wind or ice. Maybe Helen was panicking over a childhood fever or a sound outside her cousin's home. Who knew? But Nick thought it was more and that was good enough for her. And if, heaven forbid, he was right, was she going to leave him to face the consequences alone?

"I'm going with you," she said as he rolled to a stop.

"But Katie—"

She smiled as she touched his cheek. "Don't you know by now that it's pretty useless arguing with me?"

He nodded. It looked as though his eyes had watered. Turning her head to give him privacy, she said, "We only have an hour and a half before the plane leaves." She took out her cell phone and called Tess.

They made a slight detour on their way to the airport, at a shipping pier more or less abandoned in the middle of the night. Nick slipped out of the car and walked to the end of the pier. She saw him toss something toward the water, then quickly return to the car.

"Did you just get rid of Carson's gun?" Katie asked.

"I couldn't check it through with my luggage," he said, backing the car up and turning it around. "Besides, I don't want any connection between you and me and Carson. Still, that makes three guns we've dumped in Puget Sound since yesterday."

"Three guns and one body," Katie amended. "I'm beginning to feel like Bonnie and Clyde."

THE FLIGHT BACK took twice as long as the flight down to Seattle had, or so it seemed to Katie. As anxious as she had been on her mother's and Tess's behalf, she was twice as anxious now to get back to Lily. Nick had checked into some kind of combat zone. He was tense and focused and looked dangerous.

Katie hoped he wasn't having the same kind of thoughts she was having. For the first time in a day or two, she had nothing to do but think; there were things that didn't add up and she was beginning to suspect the answers were going to be devastating. But certain things made sense when looked at in the proper light. Hopefully, Nick wouldn't reach these same conclusions before he could act on them.

They landed in the early morning and took a taxi through the drizzle to the water port where Nick had left his plane. It was still several hours flying to Vixen Hills, where Helen and Lily were staying. While Nick settled his bill and did a preflight check, she camped in the phone booth and called Helen's cousin's number. Her cell phone was out of its range again. The signal was always busy. She also called her mother to explain her absence at the hospital.

Nick had written down the phone number for the police and she called that, as well. She was told the man Nick had spoken to earlier that day had gone off shift hours ago and that he'd checked on Helen and Lily on his way home.

"So, you've heard back from him?" she asked.

"Hours ago, ma'am," she was told. "He didn't find nothing out of the ordinary. He'd just put in a double shift so he was going on home to bed. It's been real windy here, though it's dying down now. Don't worry, everything is fine."

Katie reported all this to Nick, who nodded briskly and didn't look the least bit relieved.

Much to her surprise, Katie dozed during much of the flight to Vixen Hill. Nick was so tied up in knots he couldn't hold a coherent conversation and it seemed like weeks since she'd had a good night's sleep. Her head didn't hurt anymore and even her leg seldom throbbed, but her fatigue was like an unwelcome guest who wouldn't take the hint and go away.

She woke up as the plane bounced around upon landing in Vixen Hill. Her eyes few open and a rush of adrenaline left her dizzy.

Nick made arrangements with the airstrip for the loan of a four-wheel-drive Jeep. He reclaimed his rifle from the back of the plane and transferred it into the Jeep, pocketing the gun they'd left in the plane. Katie crossed her fingers they wouldn't need to use either weapon.

Thanks to the people at the airstrip, they had pretty good directions to the cousin's house and, within twenty minutes, pulled up in front of a simple green house set out on a huge parcel of land. The drapes were closed but there was a lamp burning inside. There was also a police SUV in the long driveway.

"What's he doing still here? Or did someone get called back?" Katie said.

Nick swore under his breath. "I knew something was wrong," he said, jumping out of the Jeep, the rifle in his right hand. Katie trotted along behind him. They quickly crossed the heavily shadowed yard. A figure sat in the SUV and Nick knocked on the window. When the figure didn't respond, Nick opened the driver's door.

A middle-aged man in a uniform toppled toward Nick. He had a bullet hole in the middle of his forehead.

Katie gasped.

Nick caught her hand. "Quiet…"

Gently shoving the dead man back into the SUV, Nick closed the door without making a sound. He kept Katie's hand in his and pulled her toward the house, using the coming darkness and shadows to hide their movement.

The front-room drapes were pulled, but once they got closer they could see a gap in the middle. Nick knelt down and peered through the gap as Katie examined the front door. It had looked shut tight from the street, but now that they were closer, she could see it was slightly ajar. Moving over to Nick, she leaned down and whispered in his ear. "Nick?"

He jumped back to his feet, unsettling her, catching her arms with his hands, steadying her. "Stay here," he demanded, and flinging the front door open, disappeared into the house.

"Like hell," Katie said to herself, and followed Nick inside.

The house was small and immaculate except for the pool of blood staining the beige carpet. Helen lay in this pool, her eyelids fluttering as Nick knelt over her. "Where's Lily?" he demanded. "Helen, where's Lily?"

Katie's heart pounded against her ribs. She tore off down the hall and opened every door, looking for a small, frightened child.

Erupting back into the living room a moment later, Nick said, "See if the phone works. Call nine-one-one." He held a sofa pillow against Helen's chest.

Katie found the phone off the hook. She

replaced it and was rewarded with a dial tone. As she made the call, she watched Nick trying to help Helen.

The woman's pale face was as translucent as an icicle. Her own blood, splattered onto her cheek, looked garish next to her pale skin. Katie spoke into the receiver and then joined Nick by Helen's side.

"It's my fault," Helen said, staring right into Nick's eyes.

"Shh," he said.

"Lily—"

"Where is she, Helen? Did someone take her?"

"He took her."

Helen's words hung in the air for a second.

"He?" Nick said at last.

"I don't know his name," she said haltingly. "Only a phone number. I thought…I thought I was helping."

"Helping who?" Nick said.

Katie touched his arm. This is what she'd feared, what she'd anticipated. There had to be someone on the inside and Helen was the only possibility. She said, "She thought she was helping you."

"Helping me?"

"She intercepted the wedding invitation from my mother," Katie said, staring at Helen. "The one my mother sent you without your father's permission or knowledge."

Nick glanced at Katie as though she were crazy. "She tried to hide it. So what?" he snapped.

Helen spoke again. "Weeks after Patricia died, a man came. He told me…he told me your father was responsible for her death. Patricia wouldn't have died if your father had stayed away. He'd come again and next time it would be Lily who got hurt or you…I had to stop him."

"How?" Katie said softly.

"All I had to do was watch for some sign he was coming back and pass it along to this man. He would see that your father was brought to justice for what he did to Patricia. He would keep Lily safe."

As Helen closed her eyes, Katie added, "And so when that invitation came, you passed along the return address and that's what began the current problems. Right, Helen?"

Helen's hand flopped feebly by her side. She was holding a piece of yellow paper. "I didn't know," she gasped softly, her eyes open and pleading for understanding. "I'd never hurt Lily. I didn't know."

"Where did he take her?" Nick said, his voice icy calm.

Helen whispered, "He took…cousin's truck."

"When? Where?"

"Four hours? Five?"

"Helen, where?"

Blood gurgled from the corner of her mouth. "I…I didn't know…"

Her eyes remained open, but took on the glassy stare of death.

Nick felt for a pulse, closed her eyes and took the blood-smeared paper from her hand.

His jaw tightened as he read it before handing it to Katie.

Pierce,
Your father for your daughter. Your house. No cops. You have until nine tomorrow morning and then the little girl dies.

Katie swallowed.
Nick stood abruptly. "I have to get out of

here. It'll take two hours to fly to Doc's house to get my father and then four or five to get back to Frostbite."

Katie caught his arm. "We can't do that! We can't trade your father—"

He glowered at her. "Don't start with me, Katie. This is my child. What has my father ever done to deserve to live?"

"Deserve to live? Listen to yourself. I have to tell you something—"

"I'm leaving right this moment," he interrupted. "If you're coming, come now."

And with that, he grabbed his rifle off the floor and darted from the house. Katie spied a small gray form on the carpet by the door. Picking up Lily's abandoned bunny, she hurried after Nick.

THEY PASSED emergency vehicles on the ride back to the airport where Nick had made arrangements to have the plane refueled during their absence. They were in the air in record time, headed south to Doc's place.

Katie said, "Why didn't they make Helen tell them where Doc lived? Why take Lily and risk you calling the police?"

"Helen didn't know where Doc lives. She didn't even know his last name."

Katie shook her head. "This is a trap, Nick. They could have found Doc somehow. They've been one step ahead the whole time."

"Thanks to Helen," Nick said. "I trusted that woman and all this time, she was working for the mob? Reporting to them? She must have told Carson we were going to Seattle—I fed her everything they wanted to know."

"She didn't know who she was working for. She thought your father was responsible for your wife's death and she wanted revenge."

"My father responsible? How? He was walking with Patricia. His fault was leaving her there to die alone."

"I've been trying to tell you. Back on the ferry, Carson insinuated *he* drove the car that killed your wife. I think your father recognized him and that's why he disappeared. Your father didn't want you or Lily to get hurt. He left to protect you and your daughter, to draw Carson away."

He turned to face her. "But he came back."

"I've been thinking about this. I think this is what happened. Helen alerted Carson to your father's new location and change of last name, then Carson told the mob. They waited until he and my mother made an easy target, kidnapped my mother, told your father to produce his life-insurance policy or else. It probably never occurred to them that your father would still have the money. Remember when you talked to Benito? You said he was surprised the money was still around. Anyway, Carson was sent to keep an eye on your father. Your father used the promise of the money to buy time. Carson thought he had a surefire way to make a million bucks. With your father dead, no one would know."

"So he led Carson to my house. He led him to Lily."

"He must have escaped Carson and thought he could break into your house, reclaim the disk and leave without you ever being the wiser. But Carson caught up with him and you caught up with Carson."

"And he told you all this?"

"No. I figured most of this out when I stopped to wonder who could have put the finger on your dad. He'd been missing for over two years. Helen was the only one. She hated your father with a passion."

"So did I," Nick said.

"It was your father who was supposed to die in that accident. Patricia was just an innocent bystander. He knew that, Nick. Can you imagine how guilty he's felt all this time?"

Nick closed his eyes and rubbed his forehead with his fist. "I have to return him if I'm going to save Lily," he said at last.

"No," she said, touching his shoulder, trying to make him see that he wasn't alone. She was there, and she could help if he would only allow it.

"You said Doc told you that your father couldn't travel yet. A trip like this will probably kill him, Nick. And in the end, his very presence will be a handicap, someone else for you to worry about because you know as well as I do that you aren't going to hand a wounded man to a cold-blooded killer and that even if you could, the killer would never allow you or Lily or me to walk free. Leave your father out of this."

"But Lily—"

"We'll get her," Katie said. "You'll rescue her. I have faith in you."

He was perfectly still for a moment. Katie looked out the windshield into the night. They were up above the clouds. The stars twinkled and shone as they always did. It was hard to believe evil could exist on earth when the heavens looked so peaceful and pure.

But it could and it did.

Slowly, she became aware that Nick had started a gradual turn. He was headed back to Frostbite, back to Lily.

Their eyes met and held.

Chapter Nineteen

"I'm smaller than you are," Katie said for the third time.

And for the third time Nick said, "I don't care, it's too dangerous."

"If we're going to have a future," she pronounced as they landed in Frostbite, "you're going to have to stop worrying about me."

He taxied to a halt by his hangar, turned off the engine, took off his headphones and turned to face her. "Who said anything about a future?"

"You did."

"When?"

"When you were making love to me," she said, smiling like she did, the way only she could, with her eyes twinkling with mischief and her delicious lips curved just so.

The unbearable tension that had been mounting in Nick since the moment he discovered Lily missing found a short release in Katie's wide-eyed remark. He laughed before leaning across the seat and kissing her. He said, "Don't you know never to believe a word a man tells you when he wants sex?"

She touched his face and said, "Use your head, Nick. I'm smaller."

"The door is two-feet square. Plenty of room for me."

"Not inside the actual wood room. You'd have to shuffle wood and that's too noisy. I can slip in between the stacks and through the wood door right into the living room."

The awful part of this argument was that she was right. So what? He said, "I'm not going to risk losing you."

"I'm not yours to risk or not risk," she said defiantly.

Looking into her eyes, he flashed back on making love to her just a few hours before. She'd been a passionate, generous lover, meeting him more than halfway, so open and honest that for the first time in years, he'd known who he was again.

And now she wanted to risk her life.

"Katie," he began—

"Don't say it," she said, eyes blazing. "Don't tell me to stay behind or remind me

Lily's not my problem. Just don't do that to me. Please."

He kissed her forehead. "Don't you understand?" he whispered.

She stared into his eyes. "Yes, as a matter of fact, I do, Nick. Do you?"

Temporarily lost as to what they were talking about, he muttered, "I don't—"

"Sweetheart? Just shut up, okay?" she said, and turning away, opened her door, letting a blast of frosty air into the snug cockpit.

They got out of the plane, their condensed breath all but obscuring their faces. The night was clear and there was a full moon— a stroke of luck for them, but it was cold. Nick unlocked his hangar and rolled up the door. He didn't take the time to put the plane away. There'd be time later—or things would go wrong and it simply wouldn't matter. Nothing would matter.

He strapped the rifle on the snowmobile along with the cross-country skis and poles and they were off, him driving, Katie plastered to his back. There wasn't as much snow as before and the actual roads looked navigable for a four-wheel drive. Nick thought of Helen's cousin's truck negotiating these roads with a killer behind the wheel and his three-year-old daughter asleep in the passenger seat. At least Nick hoped she'd been asleep. He hoped she hadn't seen Helen lying on the floor, dying, or heard her crying out.

He drove faster, taking the old logging road, stopping where he'd stopped before on the other side of the small bridge, anxious that neither the headlights nor the sound of the engine gave them away before they were ready.

They had each slipped a small flashlight into their pockets before leaving the plane. Nick cautioned Katie to keep the light pointed down at all times, but after a few steps, they realized the full moon created a path along the white snow that made additional light unnecessary.

He'd strapped the skis on Katie. He himself plodded through the snow, wishing he'd thought to bring snowshoes, his anxiety canceling the stress of walking, his mind trying to come up with an alternate plan that wouldn't necessitate Katie entering the lion's den.

But there wasn't one and so as smoothly as a well-tended machine switching gear, he committed himself to their plan and stopped agonizing over nonexistent choices.

They finally made it to the far side of the boathouse. From this vantage point, Nick could see the front of his house and, sure enough, a light-colored truck was parked in his driveway, which gave him a few interesting ideas when it came to creating a diversion. There were lights on within the house and wisps of smoke escaped the chimney.

After Katie took off the skis, he leaned close and whispered in her ear. "I'll give you ten minutes once we separate before I create a diversion. Remember we're not sure how many of them there are or where in the house they've stashed Lily. And as soon as you have her, get out of that house."

She nodded and started to move away and he pulled her back. Whispering against her cheek, he added, "Be careful, Katie. If anything happens to you or Lily—"

Too choked to finish his sentence, he kissed her fiercely then pushed her away, following close on her heels.

KATIE WAITED for Nick to unlock the door to the woodshed before slipping inside as he disappeared into the thick shadows. She took off her shoes and brushed off any lingering snow. The flashlight revealed the door leading to the small room that opened directly, by means of a two-foot-square door, onto the fireplace hearth.

Slowly, quietly, she let herself in that door, fighting for crawl space with several days' worth of firewood. It was a good thing Nick had finally agreed to let her do this part. His broad shoulders would never have fit without knocking things around.

Taking a deep breath, ear pressed against the small inner wood door, she waited for the sound of a diversion. She didn't have to wait long.

The explosion came from the front of the house. She heard running footsteps, alarmingly close. Shots fired. Yelling. How long to wait? The seconds passed like hours until she finally forced herself to push open the little door and tumble onto the rock hearth. The front door was wide-open, suggesting the bad guy had run outside. Katie said a silent prayer for Nick.

She was on her feet in seconds, adrenaline pushing her forward as she ran toward Lily's bedroom. Outside, visible through the windows, orange flames rocketed the night air. Katie ran down the hall, skidding on the hardwood floors in her socks as she came to Lily's open door.

Amazingly, the small child had slept

through the disruption and lay with eyes closed, peaceful and innocent and seemingly safe, blond curls framing her sweet face. Katie was halfway to the bed when she finally caught sight of the second person in the room, sitting on the other side of the bed, a gun in his lap pointed straight at Lily.

Carson.

"I killed you," she gasped, coming to an abrupt halt. Adrenaline drained from her body like wine from an uncorked bottle.

The shock of seeing him alive warred with the awful knowledge that she'd failed, that they'd failed. The killer hadn't left the house to respond to Nick's diversion—he'd come back here to Lily's room.

A bloody bandage wrapped his high forehead. Deep circles under his eyes emphasized gaunt cheeks. From his dull black hair to his wrinkled, bloodied clothes, he'd lost his polish, lost his aura of cool control and now looked like a man with absolutely nothing more to lose.

"Good thing for me you're a lousy shot," he said, his black eyes brutal. Katie didn't need to remind herself that he'd already killed at least two people. Three, if you counted Nick's late wife. "The bullet just grazed my head," he added. "We weren't far from shore and I'm a good swimmer. Hand over your weapon."

Katie put her hands out to her sides. "I don't have a weapon." She'd refused the handgun Nick had pressed on her.

"Pierce sent you in here without a gun? Not very gallant of him. I suppose he expected me to run outside when he blew up the truck?"

"I suppose," Katie said.

"I shot him from the front door," Carson said, an unholy smile stretching his thin lips. "Shot him dead. He's out there in the snow. Unlike you, I kill what I shoot at. Come over here."

Nick dead? No. She refused to believe it, and yet… didn't a part of her heart know Carson spoke the truth? Couldn't she feel a hole where once there had been the warmth and comfort of love? Had she ever really expected they would all come out of this alive? Oh, Nick!

Her chest collapsed in on itself, imploding like an old star system, dead and gone in the blink of an eye. And yet, she stood taller than ever. If Nick was gone, it was up to her to save his daughter. She crossed the room with sure steps, pausing for just an instant as she passed Lily's oversize window, catching a glimpse of the moonlit snow outside and the lake beyond, aspects of another world now, another planet, another dimension.

"Hurry up. Take off your jacket," Carson demanded as he stood.

She took off the bulky jacket and dropped it to the floor. He frisked her quickly, expertly, reminding her he was a cop or had been one. He said, "I guess Pierce found his father's embezzled money and turned it over to Benito?"

"No," she said. "I know where it is. Don't hurt Lily and it's all yours."

He laughed at her as he snapped handcuffs on her wrists. "You're in no position to bargain, lady. I'm wagering it's on Pierce's plane," he added, and then flung the small key at Lily's slumbering form. It bounced off her arm; the child didn't flinch.

Turning on Carson, Katie said, "What did you do to her?"

"Gave her a decongestant. You should thank me. She'll sleep through the whole thing."

"Did she see you shoot her babysitter or that poor cop?" Katie demanded.

"She was already asleep. Once I get rid of you and her, I'll go after Bill Thurman. I take it you didn't bring him with you. I didn't see him when I shot Pierce."

"You'll never find Nick's father without Nick," Katie said, once again leaping over the open wound of Nick's death.

"On the contrary. It wasn't hard to…persuade…the babysitter to tell me Thurman is staying at Doc's place. Not many friends earn a nickname like that. If Pierce were still alive I bet he'd be kicking himself for putting Doc in his address book. So, don't you worry, I'll get him. I always get my man."

He poked Katie with the gun. "Lay down next to the kid," he added, shoving her toward the bed as he moved in front of the window on his way to the door. He was going to execute them, together. Katie's head raced as she tried to think of a way to stop what now seemed inevitable. The cuffs were heavy on her wrists. Could she get close enough to bang him on the head with them? And the key. It was lying there on the blanket.

But there was no time.

In the next instant, she heard a shot and instinctively threw herself on top of Lily, grabbing the key as she did so. The shot was followed by the roar of breaking glass. Katie looked up in time to see Nick leap through the shattered window, rifle in hand, blood streaming down his face, one arm hanging limp and bloody.

"Nick!"

Carson lay on the floor beneath a mountain of safety glass, his head a bloody pulp.

Katie sat up as Nick crossed the room, his focus moving from her face to his daughter's still form. Horror touched his eyes. "Is she…is she hurt?"

"No, no, darling, she's fine, just drugged," Katie hastened to assure him. She sat up, cradling Lily, shaking not only from the cold air pouring through the broken window but from the culmination of the past few minutes.

Nick sat down on the bed beside her. Gently brushing Lily's hair away with his good hand, he leaned over and kissed her forehead. Then he turned his gaze to Katie. "Are you hurt?" he murmured.

As he took the key from her and freed her wrists, she grabbed a fistful of pink sheet and held it against his arm to stop the bleeding. Determined not to cry yet unable to stop the tears rolling down her cheeks, she mumbled, "I'm not hurt. But you—"

"It's nothing," he said, sliding his arm

around her shoulder, looking down at his daughter's face. They sat there for a moment in the silence, amazed to be alive, amazed to know it was finally over, that they were safe.

He kissed her gently.

"I thought you were dead," Katie said.

"It's just a flesh wound."

"But Carson…he said you were dead."

"He should have come outside and checked for sure," Nick said. "When I fell I hunkered down in the snow and just lay there. I guess I'm a better actor than I knew I was."

Katie looked from his injured arm to his blood-splattered face, into his green eyes. "I love you," she said, running a hand over his unshaven cheek. "You don't have to love me. It's okay. But I love you."

He peered at her deeply. "I knew you were going to be trouble from the first moment I saw you," he said.

"Does that mean—"

"Yes."

And he kissed her again.

Epilogue

Everything was ready.

The restaurant had been closed for the evening to host a small, private party. Security was posted at every door. The wedding couple was due to arrive at any moment.

Nick reached for Katie's hand, his thumb running over the diamond he'd placed on her finger about twelve hours after he saved her from Carson. A wide gold band sat next to it, placed there six months later, right before he sold his land and house in Alaska and bought this little beachside restaurant on Maui. Right before they moved here and started over.

Katie held Lily against her hip. Both beautiful, tanned faces reflected the coming excitement.

His gaze reached a corner table at which his

father and Katie's mother sat hand in hand, sipping champagne, watching the sunset.

"They look so content," Katie said, peering around him.

"Yes, they do. And by this time tomorrow, they'll be off somewhere living under an assumed name."

Within a few moments, Tess wafted into the restaurant in a cloud of white, Ryan Hill at her side, looking as smitten as Nick knew he'd looked at his own wedding several weeks before. As Katie hugged her sister, Nick shook Ryan's hand.

It took a little getting used to, this seeing the two women together, both blond again, both with short, sexy hair, both identical down to their expressions and the sound of their voices.

And yet infinitely different, at least to him. Tess was fine, Tess was great, but Katie—well, she took his breath away.

Katie's eyes met his at that moment and he knew she knew exactly what he was thinking. She always did.

"It's time to get started," she said, handing him Lily, then reaching up on tiptoes to brush her lips against his, turning away even as she did so.

"Not so fast," he said, pulling her back. As

Lily shrieked with laughter, he kissed Katie again, this time soundly, this time to remind her that she was his.

And that he was hers.

Forever.

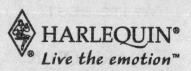

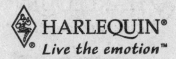

...there's more to the story!

Superromance.
A *big* satisfying read about unforgettable
characters. Each month we offer *six* very different
stories that range from family drama to adventure
and mystery, from highly emotional stories to
romantic comedies—and much more! Stories
about people you'll believe in and care about.
Stories too compelling to put down....

Our authors are among today's *best* romance
writers. You'll find familiar names and talented
newcomers. Many of them are award winners—
and you'll see why!

If you want the biggest and best
in romance fiction, you'll get it
from Superromance!

Emotional, Exciting, Unexpected...

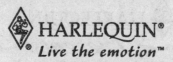

HARLEQUIN®
Presents

The world's bestselling romance series...
The series that brings you your favorite authors,
month after month:

Helen Bianchin...Emma Darcy
Lynne Graham...Penny Jordan
Miranda Lee...Sandra Marton
Anne Mather...Carole Mortimer
Susan Napier...Michelle Reid

and many more uniquely talented authors!

Wealthy, powerful, gorgeous men...
Women who have feelings just like your own...
The stories you love, set in exotic, glamorous locations...

HARLEQUIN®
Presents

Seduction and Passion Guaranteed!